"Trust me, Katy. I can sweeten the deal.

"If you sell the rights to the Baby Katy doll," Derek continued, "a lot of manufacturing contracts can be made available to the town factory."

"Oh, sure." She sighed. "More plastic hairbrushes. How creative..."

"What's more important to the town's economy? Creativity or jobs? Besides, we've neglected to mention something even more important than this little town."

"What?"

"*You*, Katy."

"What about me?"

"Why not try being just a little bit selfish?" Derek cupped a hand beneath her chin. Smiling faintly, he lifted her face to meet his gaze. "One million dollars is a lot of money. Have you ever been selfish before? It can be quite healthy sometimes, you know.... I say this for your own good."

She was lost in the silvery depths of his eyes. "And you presume to know what's good for me?"

Derek's hand traveled downward to rest on her slender waist. "I have a feeling I'd always know what was good for you...."

Dear Reader,

Welcome to Silhouette—experience the magic of the wonderful world where two people fall in love. Meet heroines that will make you cheer for their happiness, and heroes (be they the boy next door or a handsome, mysterious stranger) who will win your heart. Silhouette Romance reflects the magic of love—sweeping you away with books that will make you laugh and cry, heartwarming, poignant stories that will move you time and time again.

In the coming months we're publishing romances by many of your all-time favorites, such as Diana Palmer, Brittany Young, Sondra Stanford and Annette Broadrick. Your response to these authors and our other Silhouette Romance authors has served as a touchstone for us, and we're pleased to bring you more books with Silhouette's distinctive medley of charm, wit and—above all—*romance.*

I hope you enjoy this book and the many stories to come. Experience the magic!

Sincerely,

Tara Hughes
Senior Editor
Silhouette Books

VICTORIA GLENN

The Enchanted Summer

Silhouette Romance

Published by Silhouette Books New York

America's Publisher of Contemporary Romance

For Twinkie,
with love.

SILHOUETTE BOOKS
300 E. 42nd St., New York, N.Y. 10017

ISBN: 0-373-08652-0

First Silhouette Books printing June 1989

All the characters in this book are fictitious. Any
resemblance to actual persons, living or dead, is
purely coincidental.

Printed in the U.S.A.

Books by Victoria Glenn

Silhouette Romance

Not Meant for Love #321
Heart of Glass #362
Mermaid #386
The Matthews Affair #396
Man by the Fire #455
One of the Family #508
The Winter Heart #534
Moon in the Water #585
The Tender Tyrant #628
The Enchanted Summer #652

VICTORIA GLENN,

an award-winning writer herself, comes from a family of writers. She makes her home in the Connecticut countryside but divides her time between the East and West Coasts. She considers it essential to the creative process to visit Disneyland at least twice a year.

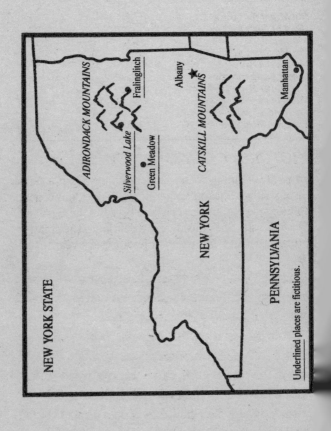

NEW YORK STATE

ADIRONDACK MOUNTAINS

Fralinglitch

Silverwood Lake

Green Meadow

Albany

CATSKILL MOUNTAINS

Manhattan

NEW YORK

PENNSYLVANIA

Underlined places are fictitious.

Chapter One

I happen to have a son who is single."

These are the nine deadliest words in the English language.

Should any proud mother smile benevolently and utter this fatal sentence, be forewarned. Run, do not walk, to the nearest emergency exit.

Tonight was a perfect example. Forget about the Black Death, the eruption of Vesuvius and the sinking of the Titanic. All those·disasters paled in comparison to Marvin Feeney, Jr. With his crumpled plaid tuxedo, greasy hair pulled back in a short ponytail, and loud, screeching laugh like a hyena, he was every unmarried woman's nightmare come true.

"So, don't I know how to show a girl a great time?" Marvin the Abominable was asking now, completely unperturbed by the clump of beluga caviar staining the front of his ruffled satin shirt.

Katy managed a feeble smile. *A great time?* Frankly, she'd rather be having a root canal. Where was a fire exit, an ejector seat or an escape pod, when a person really needed one, anyhow?

"C'mon, babe, have another drink." Marvin corralled a passing waiter and grabbed a glass of champagne from the silver tray.

"I really don't want—" she began to protest, but it was too late. Already the expensive French crystal was unceremoniously being pushed into her hand. Katy gave a sigh of utter resignation and impatiently blew a wilted strand of red hair away from her eye. Had she been alone, this might have been a reasonably pleasant evening. After all, how often did a struggling art student get the opportunity to attend such a glamorous party? Here she was, forty stories above the city in a sprawling penthouse apartment of chrome and glass. Outside, in a sweeping panorama view of Manhattan, a million lights seemed to glitter against the backdrop of the night. Back home in Green Meadow, she had grown up believing that such splendor existed only in the movies. This was an exotic and alien world. A world of wealth and privilege. It excited her artist's imagination, and made Katy wish she had brought along a sketch pad. She made a mental note to remember every detail—the lavish buffet, the celebrated twenty-piece orchestra and the tanned, elegant women in their designer gowns.

If only she could just forget the man who had brought her!

"For such a terrific-looking chick, you're really tense!" Marvin's bloodshot eyes had begun to glaze over. "Why don't you loosen up?"

Katy groaned inwardly as her companion downed yet another martini. Never, never again would she agree to meet anyone else's "wonderful son." No matter *how* lonely life in New York might be for a single woman.

This time, the invitation had seemed so harmless. Her quiet, sweet-natured neighbor, Mrs. Feeney, had rhapsodized endlessly about the virtues of her pride and joy, her son, who was a successful accountant. Somehow Katy had conjured up visions of a gentle soul with horn-rimmed glasses, scuffed wing-tipped brown oxfords and a faded corduroy sport jacket. She had expected Marvin, Jr. to be soft-spoken, shy and endearingly clumsy. Kind and unprepossessing. Just an ordinary, *nice* human being. She certainly hadn't expected The Blind Date from Hell.

"Are you going to drink that champagne, or what?" His voice grew louder and several nearby guests stared disapprovingly in their direction.

"I beg your pardon?" Katy's tone held just the right note of icy reproach. This was rapidly turning into the most embarrassing night of her life. Once again she gave an inward sigh. There was a lot to be said for staying home alone on a Saturday night doing laundry. Suddenly she envied her roommate Darlene, who right now was back at the apartment, polishing her nails and watching a Three Stooges marathon on television. It was Darlene who had lent her the stunning cocktail dress she was wearing. An aspiring fashion designer, Darlene had painstakingly hand-sewn every last stitch of the sequined sapphire-blue sheath. Strapless and spectacular, it was every bit as chic as any of the high-priced creations worn by the other guests. It clung to Katy's slender figure in all the right places, providing the perfect foil for her glossy red hair and creamy complexion. Several women had already made envious compliments in the powder room, and numerous middle-aged males continued to gaze at her in undisguised admiration. In fact, for the past hour, one man in particular had been staring quite blatantly in her direction. An essentially modest person, Katy found most of this attention rather unnerving. It did nothing to quiet the butterflies in her stomach.

"...of course, it's only fair to warn you that I'm not ready for a permanent relationship," Marvin was droning on pompously.

"*Excuse* me?" She raised an eyebrow.

"Sure, I admit most women find the whole package pretty darned desirable, and who wouldn't? A successful CPA, with his own condo on the West Side, not to mention my considerable charm and sense of style. Let's face it—" he paused significantly "—I've had to break quite a few hearts."

It was taking every last ounce of self-control not to hurl the contents of her champagne glass over Marvin Feeney's incredibly swelled head. What utter conceit! What complete arrogance! Enough of this nonsense, Katy decided firmly. There was a point of no return when a man's behavior went from obnoxious to intolerable. A decent interval had already elapsed. Marvin Feeney had been given ample opportunity to redeem himself according to every unwritten rule of blind date etiquette, and had failed miserably. It was now time to call for a taxicab, even though this was an extravagance her limited budget could ill afford. On the other hand, did a passenger on a doomed airplane stop to worry about the price of a parachute?

"Yeah, I'm in no rush for that final commitment," Marvin said, his words becoming more and more slurred. "As far as marriage is concerned, there's quite a lot of time before I settle for that old ball and chain. A guy in my position can afford to be choosy, babe."

"I'm *sure*," Katy muttered through clenched teeth. Maybe it was true about reincarnation, and she was being punished for something rotten she'd done in a previous life. Why did it seem so utterly impossible to meet a *normal* male in this town? All of her women friends seemed to be suffering the same unhappy predicament these days. There were fewer and fewer available men, and they all apparently possessed egos the size of Texas. It was becoming more and more difficult to meet a man who didn't act as if he was doing the entire female population a tremendous favor.

In the past year, since moving to New York City, nearly every date Katy had gone out on—and those were few and far between—had qualified as a major disaster. Each one seemed worse than the one before. It was absolutely disheartening. Of course, nothing had ever come close to tonight's debacle. Suddenly Katy felt an ache of homesickness for the tiny, upstate country town where she had spent most of her twenty-four years. Maybe the young men there didn't make her pulse race a mile a minute, but in Green Meadow no girl ever died of loneliness, either. Everyone had grown up together, and so when Saturday night came around, there was always something going on, even if it was as simple as a cookout at the lake, bowling, or a movie at the local drive-in. No one was ever excluded because he or she didn't have a date. Everyone was part of the gang.

Katy glanced furtively around the rambling apartment and noted with a sinking heart that every available telephone was currently occupied. On one extension, a balding, self-important businessman was talking urgently into the receiver, while in another corner of the living room, a chain-smoking actress had spent the past half hour tearfully engaged in an argument. Wonderful. At this rate, Katy would never find a phone. Then she recalled there was a doorman on duty downstairs in the lobby. Occasionally she'd noticed them standing out on the street and whistling for cabs. Yes, that was what she would do, Katy decided. She'd slip into the guest bedroom, retrieve her coat, and in another twenty minutes she would be back home with a cup of hot cocoa and the daily crossword puzzle. This date with Marvin the Abominable would be just another unpleasant memory.

Actually it took very little effort to extricate herself from the clutches of the inebriated accountant. Marvin merely shrugged and seemed content to gorge himself on more hot crab canapés. Katy had almost reached the hallway, when she accidentally brushed against a tall man in an immaculate dark tuxedo. Instantly she recognized him as the person who had been staring at her from a distance for most of the evening. He was part of a cluster of middle-aged, Wall Street executive types. Up close, however, it was obvious that despite the weariness etched in his gaunt face, the man was younger than Katy had previously thought. "Excuse me," she murmured politely, and continued on her way.

"Just a minute." His deep voice stopped Katy dead in her tracks.

She looked back at him in mild surprise, and the butterflies were fluttering in her stomach again. "Yes?"

There was something almost critical in his hooded silver gaze. "I certainly don't mean to pry," he began quietly, "but is it wise to let him drink so much?"

"Who?"

"Your boyfriend over there."

"My *what*?" Katy followed his glance in Marvin's direction, and her own green eyes widened in disbelief. Did this man actually think that Marvin the Abominable was her boyfriend? It wasn't just humiliating, it was an utter insult to good taste!

"If I were you, young lady," the man continued in a serious tone, "I'd make sure your boyfriend doesn't get behind the wheel of a car tonight."

"Would you kindly stop calling him my boyfriend?" Katy demanded irritably. She seldom lost her temper, but this intimidating stranger had somehow managed to strike a vulnerable chord.

He raised a curious eyebrow. "What would you prefer I call him, then?"

"I honestly don't care," Katy groaned in frustration.

"He *is* your boyfriend, isn't he?"

"Please, that *word*!"

"What other word might you suggest?"

"He isn't my boyfriend!"

Her companion seemed puzzled. "Well, whatever your relationship may be, I would highly recommend calling him a cab."

"Actually, I was about to call *myself* a cab," Katy found herself explaining to her interrogator.

His silver-gray eyes were clearly amused. "Oh, I'd be interested to hear about this."

It was suddenly so easy to talk to this complete stranger. "Well," she began, "did you ever have one of those nights?"

"All the time." He hesitated. "Are you having 'one of those nights' right now?"

Before Katy could answer, there was a resounding crash.

"What on earth?" She turned just in time to see Marvin collide headlong with a passing waiter. This maneuver sent glassware and dishes hurtling to the floor in a rapid succession of earsplitting smashes. Struggling to maintain his balance, the young accountant flailed his arms and staggered several steps backward. This motion caused him to careen heavily against the buffet table and topple over the immense swan-shaped ice sculpture.

What followed was a scene so reminiscent of a silent-era slapstick film that it might have been hysterically funny under any other circumstances. The head caterer and several guests rushed over to catch the giant ice bird before it shattered on the ground. They clumsily succeeded, but not before one of them skidded on the slippery floor, still wet with debris from the first accident.

When it was all over, the still-intact ice sculpture lay safely in the arms of a bewildered white-haired bank president. The stunned caterer was sprawled across the lap of a distinguished female superior court judge. The unfortunate waiter was completely doused in chocolate mousse, and Marvin? In keeping with the truly absurd nature of life, he had escaped the disaster completely unscathed.

The scene was so unbelievably bizarre that nobody in the room could do anything for a moment but stare in astonished silence. Then a hubbub broke out, as the majority of guests erupted into fits of uncontrollable laughter.

This isn't really happening, Katy pleaded silently. *This all has to be part of a dream!*

"No doubt about it," the tall stranger observed in a dry tone. "You certainly *are* having 'one of those nights.'"

Katy didn't answer. She simply continued to watch in mute disbelief as the unwitting performers in this strange spectacle were helped to their feet by other members of the crowd.

"Tell me—" her companion's lips twitched "—does this sort of thing happen to you often?"

"Absolutely not!"

"Really? I find that hard to believe."

Katy looked at him in confusion. "What exactly do you mean by that?"

"Only that a girl with your looks would probably cause a sensation, no matter where she went." Oddly enough, there was the faintest hint of cynicism in his words, making the remark sound less than complimentary.

A girl with your looks. Oh, sure. There had never been a time in Katy's life when the subject of her appearance didn't go hand in hand with some kind of criticism. "A girl with your looks should be grateful." "A girl with your looks doesn't have to worry about being smart." "A girl with your looks is always going to cause trouble." Tonight she'd already heard it from Marvin Feeney, Jr., and now from this rather overpowering man. But in truth, Katy had never considered herself to be anything special. Who cared that she had been told often enough how much she represented the ideal, all-American girl? Shiny hair, long legs, healthy smile . . . what did it matter? To her artist's eye, there was nothing commendable about facial features that society judged "perfect." In Katy's mind she was unexceptional. Uninteresting. But if she were to judge attractiveness by her own standards, then the man standing before her right now certainly qualified as exceptional without any effort. His rugged, tanned face had definite character. The aquiline nose had obviously been broken at one time, the cleft in his chin was rather pronounced, and a thin white scar arced up from his jawline to the middle of one cheek. From a purely physical standpoint, he was a most appealing individual.

"You're staring."

"Excuse me?" Katy was jarred from her thoughts.

"I said, you're staring," he repeated quietly.

A bright flush suffused her face. "Oh. Was I?"

"Yes, you were."

"Sorry." It was Katy's natural instinct to apologize, even if there was no real reason for an apology. After all, wasn't this the same man who had been watching her so intently for the past hour? "You were staring, yourself," she reminded him.

"True," he admitted with a twist of his mouth, "but then, I had something well worth staring at. Come to think of it, I still do. On the other hand—" there was an ironic pause "—what's *your* excuse?"

"I like your face," she answered simply. It was the artist inside Katy speaking, of course, in her usual honest, straightforward manner. But as far as the stranger was concerned, he could not have been more shocked if a grenade had exploded in the middle of the living room.

"You *what*?"

"I like your face," she repeated with disarming frankness. "In fact, I find it quite fascinating."

"*Fascinating?*" His silver eyes narrowed incredulously. "This is the first time I've heard an adjective like *that* describe a face like mine."

"In which case, it's my turn to say I find that hard to believe."

"Why?"

With one short word he made his confusion quite clear. And then Katy understood, even though the very idea of it astounded her. It was all there—the vulnerability, the skepticism. The man actually believed he was unattractive.

"Your face is wonderful," she declared enthusiastically. "I'd love to paint it."

A muscle in his jaw tensed. "You'd love to do what?"

"Or better yet, sketch it in charcoal."

"Are you serious?"

"Certainly."

He looked at her strangely. "What's your name?"

"Katherine." She gave a faint smile. "But everyone calls me Katy."

"Katy. Now that's a nice, old-fashioned name." There was a pause. "You don't see many young women in a dress like yours named Katy."

Her bewilderment was obvious. "Why would you say something like that?"

"As I said, Katy is an old-fashioned name." He was silent for a long moment. Finally he murmured, "My name is Derek. Derek Randall." The man extended his hand with extreme politeness.

"How do you do." Katy allowed her hand to be briefly clasped in his firm, warm grip.

Derek Randall's eyes searched her face. "Would you mind if I asked you a question?" He didn't wait for her to answer. "How long have you known him?"

"Who?"

His lips twisted disparagingly. "You know very well *who*. Feeney."

"Oh, *him*." Katy glanced ruefully in Marvin's direction. Right now he was perched precariously on the arm of a leather sofa, holding yet another drink between his chubby fingers, and attempting to croon "September Song" along with the orchestra.

Derek quirked an eyebrow. "You can't mean that you've forgotten his existence already."

"Yes, I was hoping to," came her dry response.

"You'll pardon me for saying this, Katy, but I get the impression that you're not very eager to return to the man's side."

"I'm not, and by the way, how do *you* happen to know him?"

"Actually he's my accountant."

"You're kidding!"

Derek gave an amused shrug. "Believe it or not, he's terrific at his job. I wish I could say the same about his social skills." Katy's companion ran his hand restlessly through his short, brown hair. "Which returns us to my original question. How long have you known Feeney?"

She sighed and examined her wristwatch. "Oh, about three hours."

Derek Randall registered amazement. "Three hours?"

"Does that answer your question?"

He looked at her oddly. "Yes, I believe it does."

"Let me assure you, that while three hours might not be considered a long time by normal standards, it seems like an eternity to me," Katy murmured.

"That I can well believe." He gave a thin smile. A smile that did not reach his eyes. "Don't worry about it, though. One day you'll look back on this entire night and laugh."

"I doubt it."

"Trust me. I know what I'm talking about."

"Oh, is that a fact?"

"Absolutely." He leaned his lanky frame against the richly oak-paneled wall. "I base my statement on these facts—I'm older and wiser than you are. Sometimes I think I've been around forever."

Katy pressed her lips together. "You make yourself sound like Methuselah."

A shadow passed briefly across his gaunt face. "Perhaps I *am* Methuselah. I've seen just about everything."

Chapter Two

There was an uncomfortable pause, as the soft chatter of the party swirled around Katy and Derek.

What an unusual conversation to be having with a virtual stranger, Katy marveled. Never before had she encountered a man who seemed so strong, yet at the same time so oddly vulnerable. A man who in a few words could convey both aloofness and disturbing intimacy. And something else—was it a hint of regret, or even pain?

"What are you thinking?" Derek Randall's deep voice interrupted her thoughts.

Quickly she cleared her throat. "Nothing important." Actually, Katy was remembering that in several short days she would be back home in Green

Meadow, where she had spent all the summers of her life. Back in the familiar country town that had once flourished along with her grandfather's small factory. Back at the children's camp on the lake, where she had been the arts and crafts counselor for the past six years. Back among people who had known Katy since birth. The prospect was soothing, warm and comfortable. On the other hand, there would be nothing unexpected, no tensions or mysteries. No person like Derek Randall, so unquestionably masculine and vital.

The subject of Katy's thoughts continued his own intense scrutiny. His silver-gray eyes crinkled at the corners. "Nothing, hmm?"

"Uh, actually, I was just thinking how late it is."

He folded his arms knowingly against his broad chest. "Are you as bored with this party as I am?"

She met his frank gaze. "I'm not bored. It's just time to leave." Katy had no desire to linger in any room that also held Marvin Feeney, Jr. Even thirty feet away, her date's deadly presence grated on her nerves, and Katy expected the inebriated accountant to come staggering toward her any minute. These past several minutes had all merely been a brief reprieve from his unwanted attentions. Already his eyes were squinting purposefully in her direction. The sooner she was out of here, the better. Why tempt fate?

Derek watched silently as Katy tossed her head with impatience. She seemed completely unaware of how the gesture accentuated the sensual curve of her bare shoulders, or how the red sheen of her hair glimmered in the reflected light of the chandelier directly overhead. He had known many beautiful women in his life, but she was different. He didn't know why, but there was the most curious sensation in the pit of his stomach. Then again, maybe a man wasn't supposed to understand any of it. How did it happen that he could look at this beautiful creature and feel so young, yet so old at the same time? "Listen," he said suddenly, "I'm going to make sure Feeney is safely poured into a taxicab before he does himself some serious damage. After that, can I offer you a ride home?"

Katy looked at him in surprise. "A ride?"

"Let me assure you that my car has a full tank of gas, I hold a valid driver's license issued by the state of New York, and the strongest drink I've had tonight is club soda."

"Yes, but—" She hesitated. Even though all her instincts told her she could trust this man, it was still an unbendable rule that a woman should never leave a party alone with a strange man.

"Say *yes*, Katy," her companion urged beguilingly. "Somebody's got to make sure you get home all right. It's a jungle out there, you know."

Just then, there was another resounding crash, and by now Katy knew it was unnecessary even to turn around. The source of the disturbance could only be one person. She could tell by the expression on Derek Randall's face.

"Well," he declared, "it appears that everyone's favorite CPA has just passed out on the coffee table."

A moment later, they both pressed through the crowd of curious guests who surrounded Marvin's unconscious body.

Derek leaned forward. "And I was worried he'd put up a fuss if I tried to get him into a cab. I think it's safe to say that our old buddy won't be putting up much of a fuss at all . . . will you, Feeney?"

"Is he all right?" Katy was concerned. Even though she detested him personally, Marvin was still a human being. She paused. Or *was* he?

"He'll be fine," Derek assured her with a grin. "Can't you hear him snore?"

"Is that what it is?" interjected one of the other guests. "I thought that was the air conditioning."

"You bring up an interesting point," Derek reflected. "What this man needs right now is some fresh air." In one easy motion, he reached over and hoisted Marvin's stocky body across one strong shoulder. He paused to look at Katy. "I'll wait while you get your coat."

"Now, listen—"

"Katy—" he gave a faint smile "—I can't wait too long. I'm carrying at least two hundred pounds of deadweight." There was a brief pause. "I'm going to put our friend here into a cab. Then," he added softly, "I'm taking you home."

At that point, Katy realized it was useless to argue. There was nothing more to argue about. Forget about the doomsayers and pessimists with their negative attitudes. Sooner or later a person had to begin to trust people. Even in a place like Manhattan, chivalry could still exist. It was not as obsolete as the dinosaur. And in another five minutes, as she rode the elevator down to the lobby and watched Derek Randall carry the dozing accountant effortlessly toward the massive glass doors, Katy was more convinced than ever. There *were* knights in shining armor, who still came to the assistance of damsels in distress. Well, perhaps not shining armor. These days, a knight could look just as dashing in a black tuxedo and white tie.

"You know," she murmured as they stepped outside and the doorman whistled for a taxi, "It's very thoughtful of you to look after Marvin like this."

"I'd hate for something to happen to him," he admitted wryly. "Who else would do my taxes?"

By this time, the cool night air had begun to revive Marvin. "Plenty of time . . . plenty of time . . . before that old ball and chain . . ." he was muttering.

"I think I liked him better unconscious," Katy declared.

Derek grinned, and deposited him in a waiting cab. "He'll be completely awake by the time the taxi reaches the other side of the park. In any event, I know the building complex he lives in. There are always at least two doormen on duty, twenty-four hours a day. They'll make sure he gets upstairs." He added dryly, "They'll probably even tuck him in."

Katy watched silently as the cab pulled away.

"Well." Derek turned to Katy with a thoughtful expression on his angular face. "I guess that leaves just you and me."

She lifted her face up to his. "Yes, I suppose it does." Suddenly there was a chill in the night air.

Derek was looking down at her quietly, an odd light in his eyes. "You're such a lovely young woman, Katy. I wonder if—"

Suddenly there was a shrill laugh, and then a high-pitched voice exclaimed, "Darling, there you are!" A tall, beautiful woman burst out of another taxi, dashed across the sidewalk and flung herself against Derek Randall with delighted abandon. "I've been searching for you everywhere!" She appeared to be somewhere in her early thirties, with exotic features framed by ebony hair in a striking geometric cut. A breathtaking halter gown of snow-white silk showed off her coppery tanned skin to utter perfection.

Katy watched in silence as the color seemed to drain from Derek's face. "Lorna," he rasped, "what are you doing here?"

"Trying to keep an eye on you, darling!" the woman declared sarcastically, her almond-shaped eyes flashing an unmistakable message to Katy.

"Lorna—" Derek gritted the words from between hard lips "—this isn't very funny."

Lorna ignored him, wrapping her slender arms around his waist even more possessively than before. "Don't be cross, sweetheart. I suppose I should have called and let you know I'd changed my mind, but there really wasn't any time." She kissed him, and his body tensed.

"I thought we agreed not to play any more games," he uttered in a grim tone, and deftly extricated himself from the newcomer's enthusiastic embrace.

Katy continued to watch in wordless embarrassment. There was nothing more she wanted to do at this particular moment than just melt away from the scene. Tactfully she took a few steps backward, even as Lorna glanced in her direction.

"And who is *this*, may I ask?"

With the automatic politeness that had been drummed into her since childhood, Katy found herself extending a hand. "How do you do? My name is Katherine." *Only my friends call me Katy, and you, obviously, are no friend, that's for sure!*

Lorna did not accept the extended hand, nor did she offer an introduction of her own. It was clear that the original question had been directed solely at Derek Randall. She crossed her arms impatiently and glared up at him. "What's gotten into you, anyway? Everyone was looking for you at the Hendersons' dinner party, and you never showed."

"Even if I owed you an explanation," Derek said coldly, "this is neither the time nor the place." He looked at Katy and his expression softened. "Katy, if you could just give me a minute—"

"Oh, so *that*'s how the wind blows, is it?" Lorna placed her hands on her hips and gave a caustic laugh. "Up to your old tricks again, Derek? You never *could* resist a pretty face, could you, darling?"

Why do these things always happen to me? Katy wondered with a mixture of mortification and weariness. As if the excruciating three hours with Marvin the Abominable weren't enough, she now found herself in the middle of a rather sticky lovers' quarrel! Oh, the joys of being a single woman in New York City! All she wanted to do right now was make a quick getaway. "Well," she uttered shakily, "it's been charming meeting both of you, but I really must be running along!"

"Oh, what a shame!" Lorna rolled her eyes.

"Katy, wait!" Derek repeated urgently.

But she continued to walk away with deliberate swiftness and, much to her relief, he made no attempt to follow her. Just at that moment, another cab came to a stop by the curb, discharging several well-dressed passengers directly in front of her. As Katy slid hastily into the vacant taxi and slammed the door shut, she was vaguely aware of Derek Randall calling out her name for a third time. If she had looked into the rear-view mirror, Katy would perhaps have seen Derek's

jaw tighten, as he silently watched the cab disappear
into the night. But all Katy could think of was that
there weren't really any knights in shining armor, and
that this man was no different from other men, after
all. It was the oddest sensation of disappointment
she'd ever experienced.

But had Katy been able to turn around and see the
expression on Derek Randall's face, it would have
been enough to take her breath away.

By the time Katy took the train back to Green
Meadow, both Marvin Feeney and Derek Randall had
ceased to be anything but dimly disturbing memories.
With each passing day, both men became less and less
real. Somehow, through distance and time, the image
of Marvin was not quite so obnoxious, and by the
same token, Derek Randall was nothing more than an
ordinary man. Katy became convinced that everything that had seemed so intriguing, so overwhelmingly *male* about Mr. Randall was simply a product of
wishful thinking, of seeing what she had *wanted* to
see. Sure, given the situation, any man would have
seemed attractive and gallant in comparison to Marvin Feeney. In truth, however, Katy now realized that
with her usual overactive imagination, she had attri-
buted extraordinary qualities to a rather ordinary individual. Beneath the appealing surface, Derek
Randall was just another big-city bachelor with a rov-
ing eye. Even after her rather limited experience with

the opposite sex, Katy admitted that her original instincts about the man had been wrong. Derek Randall was not a man she could trust. Lord only knew what trouble she might have found herself in had his girlfriend, Lorna, not appeared so abruptly on the scene.

No, she thought resignedly, as the train wound its way northward through the lush green foliage of the Hudson Valley, why not just try to get the entire disaster out of her mind? She would never, not in a million years, understand the human male and whatever bizarre machinery made him tick. Anyway, why should she carry on like this? Had she really expected to meet a man and fall in love in that town? Her sole purpose in struggling through classes and holding down a waitress's job had been to receive a degree in fine arts. A year ago, New York City, with its magnificent museums and spectacular private galleries, had seemed like a mecca to Katy. Her anticipation of life in such a cultural haven had been intense. But now, all she could think of was that even in a city with millions of people, it was so easy to feel terribly alone. Isolated.

For a few short months, it would be delicious to forget that such a high-stress place even existed. Until September, there was no such place as Manhattan. Her half of the dingy Greenwich Village apartment had been sublet to Darlene's cousin, a summer intern at a Madison Avenue law firm. So to all intents and purposes, the apartment did not exist, either. And, Katy reminded herself forcefully, Derek Randall did not exist at all. So why on earth did the man keep creeping back into her thoughts?

Well, never mind, she decided with a sigh. In just a few more hours, she would finally be back where she belonged. Even if only for the summer. And nothing and no one, especially Derek Randall, could possibly intrude into the remote, private world that was Green Meadow.

Katy had no idea just how wrong she was.

Chapter Three

I hope you're back to stay," Leo Kruger grumbled when he met her at the train station.

Katy suppressed a laugh. He said the same thing every time she returned home for a visit. "No, Gramps." She kissed his crinkled cheek with affection. "The term starts up again at the end of August."

The elderly man gave a disdainful frown, and effortlessly tossed Katy's suitcase into the rear of the station wagon. "I still don't see why you have to go back to the city," he insisted.

"So, what's happening with the factory?" Katy asked deliberately.

"Are you changing the subject, young lady?"

"Yes."

There was a pause. "What's happening with the factory? Nothing new. Just hanging on... like yesterday, and the day before."

The sadness was evident in Leo Kruger's voice. A robust man in his late seventies, he had single-handedly built a toy company that in better times had been the lifeblood of Green Meadow. The man was that rare combination of whimsical creator and shrewd, practical businessman. Although it had been nearly ten years since the last doll had come down the production line at the Kruger Toy Works, he had found other ways for the factory to survive. In that sense, his stubborn resilience was a blessing. On the other hand, that same stubbornness was occasionally a problem for his only grandchild. Long ago, Leo Kruger had gotten the idea into his head that the only road to contentment for Katy was for her to be married with a family of her own. By the time she was eighteen, he had already decided on the perfect candidate for the position of bridegroom.

"J.B. asked about you again," the old man announced as he guided the car along the winding country road toward the village.

"That's nice," Katy murmured vaguely, and tried to concentrate on the passing scenery.

"Yes, J.B. asks about you all the time," Leo Kruger noted with a conspiratorial smile. "Just yesterday I was down at the filling station, and he happened to stop by in his patrol car...and well, what can I say? That young man's face just lit up like a Christmas tree when I mentioned you were coming home today.''

Katy didn't answer. There had been a time when she had entertained rather a strong crush on J. B. Halloran, the local sheriff. With his athletic, blond good looks, he had seemed the answer to every teenage girl's dreams. But that had been years ago, and Katy was no longer the callow fifteen-year-old who'd marveled with her other female classmates at J.B.'s uncanny resemblance to a certain Hollywood superstar. No, she thought. Nowadays, it seemed that all Katy could think about was a magnetic dark-haired person she had met at a party in a Manhattan penthouse. Despite all her best intentions, Katy had been unable to keep the disturbing image of Derek Randall out of her mind these past few days. The memory of that brief encounter still lingered.

"That's right," her grandfather continued amiably, "that young man's face just lit up when I mentioned your name, honey! Now, believe me, you could do a lot worse than marry J.B."

"Gramps, please! Don't start *that* again!"

"Start *what* again?"

Katy compressed her lips. "Stop trying to match me up with J. B. Halloran."

"And what, may I ask, is wrong with J.B.? Might I remind you that his dad and I were best friends? If

Otis were alive today, it would surely warm his heart to see our two families joined together—"

"I'm *sure*." Katy rolled her eyes. If there was one thing that her grandfather knew how to do very well, it was to inject that tone of sentimentality into his words. This succeeded in making anyone who refused his requests seem hard-hearted and cruel. Or at least feel guilty, even if there was nothing to feel guilty about.

"Okay, so maybe J.B. doesn't talk much. Maybe he's not much on words. I thought you young women these days preferred the strong, silent type."

She gave a groan. "I don't prefer *any* type. I'm not ready to get married, all right? I'm in school—"

Leo Kruger guffawed. "Since when is school more important than family? And where are you going to find a better man than J.B.? Besides, with both of your looks, think of the incredibly beautiful children you'd have." He paused significantly. "*My* great-grandchildren."

Katy sighed in resignation. What was the use of arguing? Once her grandfather got a certain idea into his head, there was no dissuading him. Silent for the rest of the ride home, she let him ramble on and on about the virtues of J.B., the late Otis, and the entire Halloran family since the war of 1812. All the time, however, Katy continued to stare out of the passenger window at the rolling green hills, so fresh with the promise of early June.

How could the concrete and glass canyons of New York City compare to the lush yet simple beauty bestowed by nature? Up here, so little had altered over the years. There still were the apple orchards, the endless pastures dotted with grazing cows, and everywhere, as they had done during Katy's childhood, wild blueberry and raspberry bushes bloomed.

Yes, she sighed again. Green Meadow was so lovely, so unchanged. So reassuring. And yet it had not been enough to keep her here. A vital ingredient had always been missing. Katy wasn't quite sure what that vital ingredient was, but she knew for certain that it had nothing to do with J.B. If something had been meant to happen between the two of them, it would have happened long ago. Somehow, though, when the enigmatic young sheriff of Green Meadow looked at her, Katy had never felt connected. There had been admiration and even warmth in his eyes, but never intimacy. Unlike—oh, great! Here she was, comparing him to Derek Randall. A man she had scarcely spent half an hour with, a man who was quite obviously involved with a more sophisticated woman. Recalling that awkward encounter with the glossy Lorna, so confident and possessive in her relationship with a man, Katy experienced a residual twinge of embarrassment. Still, as unsettling as it was to admit the fact, meeting Derek had had a profound effect on her. Those few brief moments alone with the man had been quite startling. He had been a virtual stranger, yet he seemed to know her. He was in many ways the opposite of J. B. Halloran. Derek was somehow able to evoke a sense of intimacy while maintaining his natural aloofness. Even now, thinking about him gave Katy an odd sensation in the pit of her stomach.

The station wagon lurched to a stop in the driveway of the Kruger home. Katy's entire being was flooded with warmth as she gazed up at the rambling, pink Victorian house. Coming back home always gave her such a good feeling. There it stood, as it had for nearly a century, on the rise of the hill, surrounded by chestnut trees. With its elaborate white lacelike gingerbread trim, diamond-paned windows and double cupolas, the turn-of-the-century residence resembled something out of a storybook. More than fifty years ago, Leo Kruger and his young wife had moved into this house, a gift from the bridegroom's parents. Over the years, the Kruger family had bestowed upon the structure all their cherished imagination. To Katy, growing up in her grandparents' home had been like living with Mr. and Mrs. Santa Claus. The interior of the house was an eclectic but happy jumble of bright quilts, cushions and antique furniture. Most of the time, the place was strewn with half-finished toys that Leo was designing, and Katy smiled wistfully to herself. In what other home did the wife have to continually lecture not her children, but her *husband* about leaving his toys on the floor? And what other home always seemed to look like Santa's workshop at Christmastime?

"Don't forget the town picnic tomorrow," Leo Kruger reminded her with a wink as he bounded up the winding staircase with Katy's suitcase, before she could even protest that it was far too heavy. Where did the man get his inexhaustible supply of energy from? Even with the near-hopeless state of affairs concerning the factory, Leo was the same purposeful and lively man now as he had been when the Kruger Toy Works had been at the zenith of its success, and Green Meadow's main employer. Those golden times were long gone, for with each passing day, the factory hovered closer to the brink of bankruptcy. But Leo Kruger was essentially an optimist. He simply refused to lose all hope, even though the business outlook seemed bleak. The demand for the delightfully distinctive Kruger dolls and hand-detailed cars and toy trucks would return, eventually. In the meantime, he kept the company—and the local economy—alive by taking on subcontracts to manufacture items that bore no relationship to the toy business.

"What's coming off the assembly line this month?" Katy asked her grandfather as she kicked off her sneakers and settled into the cozy window seat.

He gave a shrug and glanced around the bedroom, still unchanged since Katy's childhood. There were at least sixty or seventy dolls propped up along the numerous shelves and against the delicately rosebud-patterned walls. "This month?" he repeated almost to himself. "We're handling a cosmetic corporation's overflow orders for plastic combs and barrettes." Almost absently, Leo Kruger picked up a nearby baby doll. It bore a striking resemblance to his granddaughter that was more than coincidental. The most successful dolls of the Kruger line had been modeled after Katy during various stages of her childhood. With gentle hands, he put the toy back on the shelf. "Next month, they may subcontract us for bobby pins and curlers."

He made it sound so cheerful, but inside, Katy knew her grandfather longed for the good old days of manufacturing products that he *himself* had designed under his own company logo. She wished there was something she could do to bring back those prosperous days to Green Meadow and the factory, but Katy never had acquired the knack for business. She often wished she had inherited the old man's keen business acumen. Perhaps, if she had been born a boy... But no, that was all a lot of male chauvinist drivel, Katy decided. Still, she couldn't help feeling that in some way she had failed her grandfather. If only she had some kind of magic wand to wave over the town and the factory and make everything better.

Late into the night, Katy sat huddled up in that window seat, lost in thought. Why was she so ineffectual? Why couldn't she be more hard-driving and forceful? According to all the advice books these days, it was the aggressive person who achieved success. People like Marvin Feeney, Jr. And according to the books, one also had to be aggressive when it came to matters of the heart. Well, never having been in love, Katy didn't know much about that, but she was willing to bet that the exotic Lorna was a perfect example. There was a woman who most definitely knew what she wanted and how to go after it. Katy twisted her lips ironically, remembering the older woman's long fingernails against Derek Randall's tuxedo sleeve. Lorna also knew how to *keep* what she wanted, once she had it.

It would be several weeks before the season started at Camp Silverwood, located beside a scenic mountain lake just twenty miles from Green Meadow. In the meantime, Katy was delighted to relax and unwind a bit before her summer duties began. It had been a strenuous year with classes and a waitressing job that kept her on her feet until all hours. Now, on her second day home, the annual town picnic was a wonderful opportunity to have some fun and see all her old friends again.

As usual, the village square was closed to traffic, and the familiar yellow-and-white-striped tents were set up on the green. The Green Meadow Volunteer Fire Department Band was playing in its distinctively off-key style, balloons and streamers hung from every street sign and utility pole, and the aroma of grilled hot dogs, hamburgers and corn on the cob filled the air. No one in Green Meadow ever missed the town picnic unless they were on their deathbed, and even then it was still considered unusual to stay away. The picnic was one of the premier social events of the year, and Katy was hard-pressed to think of any other event that so typified the spirit and personality of her hometown. Everywhere she walked, Katy was greeted with smiles or hugs, as if she were a long-lost cousin.

"Welcome back, dear!" old Myrtle Hayes declared. "Have a slice of my delicious chocolate cake. You're too thin! What do they feed you in New York City?"

"Katy, don't listen to Myrtle. You're perfect!" interjected Lottie Newmeyer. "Besides, *my* chocolate cake is what you *really* will enjoy!"

"Never mind those two old biddies." Winifred Pym waved a quivering, blue-veined hand with all the superiority the eldest of the trio could muster. "*I* use only butter in my layers."

"And you are saying *I* don't?" demanded Myrtle.

"We all *know* who uses vegetable shortening, now don't we?" Lottie chimed in smugly.

Finally, Katy had to agree to take a slice of each and praised them all to the skies. When she walked away, it was with a chuckle. The same thing happened every year. The three widows had been competing with each other since girlhood. At varying stages of their lives, the competition had entailed first toys, then clothes, and then boys. But everyone in the county had to admit that none of these rivalries could hold a candle to the intensity of the annual chocolate cake wars.

Most of Katy's high school friends had stayed on in town after graduation, and they all wanted to hear about New York City.

"I hear you've got your own town house!" exclaimed Ida Johnson enviously.

"And your own private elevator," added Tim Levy with a sigh.

"Who told you *that*?" Katy rolled her eyes.

"Well, it's true, isn't it?" chirped up Jane and Elaine Torbor. Since they were children, the identical twin sisters always seemed to think and talk alike. It had often been jokingly said that the Torbor twins must share the same brain, because they always spoke in tandem. In fact, if the two of them weren't married yet, it was only because they hadn't yet met the right set of identical twin men.

"Listen, you guys—" Katy sighed "—I live in a town house, that's true, but there isn't an elevator, and my apartment is the size of a lima bean. We've got cockroaches and peeling paint, and every morning at six-thirty, there's a symphony of garbage trucks and car horns outside my window."

"Yeah, you're sure lucky," said Ida wistfully.

"At least they don't roll up the sidewalks at nine o'clock, the way they do here," observed Tim. A good-natured bean pole of a young man, he had been captain of the basketball team, and was now an assistant coach at the high school. At the age of ten, moreover, he had made an early display of his skill at the hoop by hitting both Torbor twins from a distance of twenty feet with the same water balloon.

"Anyway, we're just glad you're back," declared Jane.

"Because things get pretty boring around here without you . . ." added Elaine.

" . . . and it's great when the whole gang can get together in the summertime," finished her sister. "Just like the old days."

The old days, thought Katy with a twinge of wistfulness. How she missed them. Oh, the town was still a warm and wonderful place to live, that much was certain. From the pastel-colored buildings that lined Main Street to a town ordinance that actually forbade the issuing of minor traffic citations on a driver's birthday, there was no place quite so whimsical or kind-natured. But back when the Kruger Works still made toys, there had also been that indefinable aura of prosperity in Green Meadow. More of a lilt in people's steps. There had been a sense of pride in turning out a well-made toy or sewing a party dress for the doll line. Sure, there was still some work at the factory, but somehow it just wasn't the same. Plastic hair combs, personalized plastic pens, nameplates and party supplies were not Kruger Toys.

"Katy," said a voice behind her, "it's good to see you."

She turned around. "Hi, J.B."

The young sheriff of Green Meadow looked exceedingly dashing in his crisp summerweight khaki uniform and aviator lenses, with his blond hair bleached even lighter from the sun. Strange. Katy felt no twinge of excitement when she gazed up at this handsome friend. No tingle. He was just good old J.B., the town football hero who had come home from a tour of duty in the Marine Corps with a tired, distant look in his blue eyes. The faraway look. It seldom faded from his face, these days. He always seemed to be somewhere else. Preoccupied.

"Your grandfather told me you were coming back." He smiled and gave her shoulder an affectionate tap.

"I'm back every summer," Katy reminded him.

"One of these summers you won't come back." J.B. shook his head quietly.

"What makes you say that?"

He shrugged. "I know, Katy. I just know."

"Oh, come on, J.B.! Since when did you start reading tea leaves?" She crossed her arms and stared back at him questioningly. Why did he always have to sound so serious? He couldn't be more than five or six years older than herself, yet every time Katy encountered him on her visits home, J. B. Halloran seemed to be lapsing deeper and deeper into an early middle age.

"You're looking for something, Katy."

"Oh, and what am I looking for?"

J.B. smiled his usual thin, enigmatic smile. "I don't know. Maybe the same thing I'm looking for. Whatever it is, I doubt either of us will ever find it in Green Meadow."

"Find *what*, J.B.?"

He slowly replaced the sunglasses on the bridge of his nose. "I'm not sure, Katy. People like you and me, that certain 'thing' we look for...well, it's hard to identify. Maybe it doesn't even exist." He paused. "Maybe people like you and me should stop looking for that elusive dream, and settle for what's real."

"In other words?"

"How about a movie tonight?"

Katy nodded. "Sure, J.B."

"Oh, be still, my beating heart!" murmured Ida as J.B. walked back across the green toward his patrol car. "The hunkiest hunk in town, and he's all yours!"

"Oh, come on, Ida," she protested, "it's only a movie."

"Katy Kruger, what do you mean 'it's only a movie'? J. B. Halloran's been back for three years and he's never taken anybody to a movie. Or anywhere else, for that matter." Ida sighed. "I'm so jealous, I could die."

"We're just friends," Katy insisted.

"I wish J.B. would *arrest* me sometime," Jane declared.

"Or *me*," Elaine added.

What was the use of trying to explain to her friends that there was far less there than met the eye? Katy did not have the slightest romantic attachment to J. B. Halloran. He seemed so remote, so defeated, as if the man lacked that core of inner vitality. A vitality she had sensed inside Derek Randall.

Oh, for goodness' sake! Katy chastised herself for the hundredth time. Was she ever going to forget that smooth-talking Manhattan playboy? J.B. might not light any sparks in her heart, but at least he was honest and open. Why *shouldn't* she go out with him? Even if J.B. considered the movies to be an actual date, why was that so bad? At least they were friends. And even if something went wrong, the two of them would *still* be friends. A date with J. B. Halloran? Sure, why not? At least it would make her grandfather happy. Besides, Katy thought with a cynical grin, if she could go out on a date with Marvin Feeney, Jr., she could go out with anybody. A movie with J.B. would be duck soup.

Chapter Four

To say that it had been a difficult week for Derek Randall would have been an understatement. As an executive vice president at Consolidated Industries, he was used to hard work and long hours. He was used to dealing with impossible people and no-win situations. If some of his more envious colleagues accused him of being too hard-driving and ruthless, well, it wasn't his problem. At the age of thirty-five, Derek had no intention of changing any aspect of his personality. Not when he had risen so far on the corporate ladder. Why tamper with success? But something had happened in recent days, something so unexpected that it had thrown him off his stride. Derek Randall wasn't the kind of man to become obsessed with one particular woman. In the past, he had merely considered them to be alternately delightful and irritating creatures. He had known numerous women as lovers, but very few as friends. Just as he treated all other aspects of his life, Derek had found it simple enough to compartmentalize so-called "romance." It had its own time and place—out of sight, out of mind—which was fine with him. That was pretty much how it had always been. And then, completely out of the blue, he had encountered a girl named Katy.

The intercom buzzer shattered his reverie. Annoyed, he lifted the receiver. "Yes, Miss Jordon?"

"The conference is in five minutes, Mr. Randall," the nasal voice of his secretary informed him.

"Thank you." He replaced the receiver, and stared out his forty-seventh floor office window with its stunning view of New York harbor.

Katy. He couldn't get her out of his mind.

Derek hadn't even wanted to go to that party in the first place. In fact, he'd gone rather reluctantly, intending to put in a brief appearance along with some of his colleagues, and then make his escape. But then he'd seen a girl with red hair and beautiful eyes. It had been a long time since he could remember being affected by a woman that way. He'd forgotten what a delicious sensation it was to be hit right between the eyes, to be struck so viscerally. Especially by someone so young and sweet. That was what it was about her that Derek had found so disconcerting. He had never known any woman before who radiated such a gentle glow. It was a quality so strange, so very alien to him. He had never experienced sweetness at such a close range before. Not even as a child. Derek's eyes darkened. *Especially* not as a child. But he pushed those bitter thoughts away, in favor of something far more pleasurable. How he'd gone on staring at Katy for at least an hour at that party, unable to believe that someone like her would be caught dead with a character like Feeney.

At least, though, old Marvin had played right into his hands by getting himself completely plastered. Derek shook his head with contempt at the recollection. How could any man make such an appalling spectacle of himself, when he had a companion as exquisite as Katy? Where were that idiot's priorities? On the other hand, his accountant's disgraceful behavior had provided Derek with the opportunity to spirit Katy away for himself. He'd actually managed to win the lovely creature over with very little effort. In another few minutes, the two of them would have been driving back to her place in his car.

And who knows what might have happened then? Derek felt a curious tingling all over his lean, tall body. Just anticipating what *might* have been with Katy was having the strangest effect on him, even now. If it hadn't been for fate and its cruel tricks, the evening might have had a completely different ending.

Damn Lorna! Even now, Derek couldn't seem to recall what he'd ever seen in the woman. She was so cold, so calculating. Perhaps he'd allowed himself to fall into their brief and ultimately unsatisfying affair, because he had never really wanted to become involved. To lose control. With Lorna Daniels, he thought he'd discovered a sophistication and cynicism that matched his own. The one thing Derek hadn't counted on, though, was her intensely possessive nature. When she had appeared on the scene so unexpectedly and shattered his idyll with Katy, Derek had had to force himself not to throttle Lorna. But what had been even more difficult was forcing himself not to run after Katy. She had seemed so bewildered, so embarrassed. Derek had never run after a woman before, but for the first time, he had actually wanted to throw himself in front of her taxicab to prevent her leaving without him. What had stopped him? What had he been so afraid of? Why had he hesitated for those few crucial seconds? Then it had been too late.

For the past week, every time he tried to concentrate on business, his mind kept conjuring up Katy's face. Damn! He didn't even know her last name! He'd tried calling Feeney the next day to pump him for information, but as luck would have it, his accountant had already left, hangover and all, for a two-week retreat somewhere in the Caribbean. Derek wondered how he was going to survive for another seven days, until Marvin came back and provided him with the information he was aching to learn. Mainly, what the hell was Katy's last name, and how on earth could he find her?

Somewhere in New York was a lovely creature he couldn't stop thinking about. It made Derek grit his teeth to imagine her going out on Saturday night with any man except himself!

But fate had not yet finished playing its tricks. This time, however, the trick was anything but cruel, although Derek had no way of knowing this. It all started at the executive board meeting.

"I agree with the figures provided by our marketing division," continued Morgan Strickland, the silver-haired president of Consolidated Industries. "The current trend toward nostalgia items is on the upswing. That's where *you* come in, Derek. We've got a rather stubborn character upstate, who needs a little bit of 'friendly' persuasion."

"If you mean that toy company—" Derek shook his head "—I don't consider it a very sound investment."

The VP of Marketing almost glared at him. "Nobody wants to buy the factory, Derek. The rights to the Baby Katy are all we want."

Derek sighed inwardly. How could he escape it? Katy's name even cropped up at board meetings! "I'm quite aware you're not interested in the factory, Les."

He gave the marketing VP his coldest stare, a look that was known to wither his most self-confident colleagues. "I repeat, I don't consider it a wise investment. As it is, the toy market is glutted, not to mention unstable."

"Give this a chance, Derek," interjected Morgan genially. "Once we acquire the rights from this Kruger fellow, we can mass-produce the doll in Hong Kong and do a full-saturation media campaign in time for next Christmas."

"I honestly don't—" Derek stopped himself. Why was he protesting? Just because he had rather a strong personal prejudice against toys in general was no reason to kick up such a fuss. He'd already spoken up and expressed his opinion. A year from now, when this latest scheme from the marketing division had fallen flat on its face, he would at least have gone on record as having opposed it from the start. He cleared his throat and leaned back in the plush leather chair. "About this man Kruger—"

"He's giving us a lot of trouble," interrupted Lester Winters. "He doesn't want to sell."

"How much are we willing to offer him?" Derek looked at the man at the head of the table.

"I rely on your discretion, as always." The president smiled. "But if it comes down to it, you might have to play hardball."

"No problem." Derek rose to his feet. "Hardball is a game I've always enjoyed. I'll fly up there tomorrow."

"I knew I could count on you, Derek."

Actually, Morgan Strickland had no idea what was going on in his favorite vice president's mind at that moment. If he had, he would have been quite surprised. Derek was thinking that a brief trip up to the boondocks of New York State might be the best thing he could do right now. A little business hardball was just the thing to take his mind off a certain distraction... one that was wreaking havoc on his well-organized, carefully controlled life.

"What's the name of that hick town, again?" he asked Les Winters.

"Green Meadow." The man gave a deprecating sneer. "Can't you almost hear the cows moo?"

"Green Meadow," Derek repeated aloud. The Katy doll, he thought to himself. He was being sent to acquire a doll named *Katy*. He thought of another Katy. A vivacious, adorable redhead, who was quite a doll herself. He sighed wearily, and wished he was on his way to acquire the real, live, breathing Katy.

When he was conducting business discreetly for Consolidated Industries, Derek found it prudent to operate with the lowest possible profile. Instead of flying up to the general aviation airport outside Green Meadow in one of the small corporate jets, Derek decided to take a regularly scheduled flight to Albany and rent a car there. Then he drove the rest of the way to Green Meadow.

As he guided the beige Buick Regal along the winding country roads, he had to admit that Les Winters was right. He could hear the cows mooing without even seeing them. The area was pretty enough, almost like a picture book, with those rolling pastures and lush trees. That is, if you liked that sort of thing. Derek had never spent much time in the country. He'd been born in the city and was used to the conveniences of urban living. He also found the tranquillity of a rural environment to be no match for the tension of Manhattan. It was a tension that raced through his veins and made him feel alive and vital. As attractive as Green Meadow and its environs might be, its pastoral charm was no substitute for the allure of a city.

Suddenly he heard a siren behind him. In the rearview mirror, Derek could see the flashing blue and red lights of a patrol car. Wonderful. He shook his head in annoyance. All he needed now was an encounter with some redneck police officer. Derek had heard numerous horror stories, about how certain remote country towns made most of their money from speed traps, set up to catch unsuspecting motorists. He reached into his pockets for his driver's license, leaned back in his seat and waited for the worst.

The trooper who walked over to the Buick looked more a Hollywood actor than a redneck cop. He was tall, well built and had the sun-bleached hair of a California surfer. He took off his mirrored sunglasses and motioned for Derek to roll down his window.

Derek twisted his lips cynically and obliged. "Yes, officer?" he inquired with uncharacteristic deference.

"Are you aware, sir, that you are traveling in excess of the posted speed limit?"

"And what posted limit is that?" Derek countered with forced politeness. Who was this country cop trying to kid?

The blond giant looked around and scratched his head thoughtfully. "I guess the sign must have blown over in that thunderstorm we had last night. What a downpour *that* was, I'm here to tell you! It washed out the bridge to Silverwood Lake and drowned two of Jake Torbor's calves, when they got caught in the gully...."

"What, may I ask, is the posted limit?" Derek repeated with thinly veiled impatience.

"Twenty-five miles an hour."

"Twenty-five miles an hour seems very...low." Derek's voice now had an edge that his colleagues would have recognized as being ominous.

"It's on account of old Lottie Newmeyer's horses. Cars make them pretty jittery."

Derek groaned inwardly. What was he in the midst of now? *The Farmer in the Dell?*

"In any event," the towering police officer concluded, "I clocked you at thirty-eight miles an hour. If I might see your operator's license, sir."

Fine, just give me the damn ticket and let me go on my way! Derek muttered silently as he handed over his driver's license.

The young officer in his crisp khaki uniform studied the small document for a moment, and then an odd grin appeared on his face. "Oh, well, this changes things, Mr. Randall. There's no way I can issue you a ticket now."

"I *beg* your pardon?"

"According to this license, today is your birthday. So just forget the citation—" he ripped the paper out of his ticket book "—but keep to the posted limit until you round that next hill over there."

Derek stared in amazement, as his license was returned to him. "Sure, no problem," he muttered. What kind of a crazy town was Green Meadow?

"And Mr. Randall—" the officer continued to smile "—have a happy birthday." Then he strode back to his white patrol car and drove off in the opposite direction.

Derek just watched the patrol car disappear in the distance and shook his head. If the local cops were this nutty, what on earth could he expect from Mr. Leo Kruger?

* * *

"I've already told your representatives," the elderly man was saying to Derek Randall, "I'm not interested. I wasn't interested last week, and I'm not interested now."

The two of them were sitting in the parlor of the bizarre pink Victorian monstrosity that passed for the most elegant residence in Green Meadow. Armed with a local road map and Leo Kruger's address, Derek had proceeded directly to the factory owner's home. He hadn't yet bothered to check into a hotel or even grab a bite to eat. Derek was impatient to conduct his business and not waste any time with nonessentials.

He was somewhat taken aback, however, when Leo Kruger himself answered the doorbell. The wiry old man didn't appear to have any servants, and Derek was a bit disconcerted at the lack of formality. Although his visit had been unexpected, he still had anticipated having to deal with Leo Kruger through intermediaries. In any event, while Derek had expected some resistance from the toy manufacturer, he hadn't anticipated the strength of Leo Kruger's convictions. The old man actually considered Consolidated's rather generous offer as an insult.

"Why on earth, Mr. Randall, would I want to give your corporation the copyright to my most successful doll?"

Derek had eased himself into one of the maple rocking chairs with soft quilted cushions and smiled confidently. "If it's more money you want, Mr. Kruger, I'm quite willing to increase our already substantial offer. This will entitle you to a percentage of the Baby Katy profits—"

"Forget it, city boy. You obviously don't have the faintest idea what the heck I'm talking about." Leo Kruger rose to his feet. "So stop spinning your wheels and quoting meaningless figures at me. You're just wasting time."

Derek Randall felt like a youngster who had misbehaved in the schoolroom. No one had ever chastised him like this before, at least not in recent memory. It was something he was definitely unaccustomed to. For the first time in his highly successful career, Derek was unsure what to do next.

He cleared his throat and assumed his most intimidating tone. "Let's be blunt, Mr. Kruger. You've received numerous contracts for various plastic products from a certain cosmetic company. This company happens to be a subsidiary of Consolidated Industries."

"Are you threatening me, Mr. Randall?" Leo Kruger's hazel eyes narrowed.

Derek shrugged. "Business is so unpredictable these days. Contracts can suddenly be canceled."

"You *are* threatening me." The old man's voice grew tense.

He was so obviously upset that Derek felt a pang of guilt at his tactics. It had never particularly bothered him before, but the obvious vulnerability of the older man was oddly poignant. In a more beguiling tone, Derek said, "I know business has been difficult, Mr. Kruger. Please believe me when I tell you that Consolidated is willing to offer you, cash in hand, one million dollars for the copyright. Think of what that money could mean for you and your family. And that's just for a start. We would be willing to subcontract for even more business through our subsidiaries." Derek waited.

Leo Kruger was silent for a moment, then exhaled sharply. "It isn't my decision to make, young man. The rights to the doll no longer belong to me."

"What?" Derek sat bolt upright. This was something he hadn't expected. "Who *do* the rights belong to, then?"

"My granddaughter."

"Your *granddaughter*?"

"You know, of course, that my granddaughter was the original inspiration for the Baby Katy, and in fact, for many of my other dolls."

"No, I didn't."

"Why else would I name the doll after her?" Leo Kruger looked impatient.

"Are you saying that your granddaughter is called Katy?" Derek Randall felt submerged in a veritable sea of Katies. That name again! How on earth was he supposed to keep his mind on business? "Where can I find her?"

"Where?" The other man shrugged and gestured in the direction of the front door. "I believe she's just pulled into the driveway. I'll introduce you in a minute."

Derek gave a nod of satisfaction. Things were going just fine. How difficult would it be to negotiate a deal with a naive country girl?

A moment later, light footsteps came bounding up the porch, and an oddly familiar voice called out, "Gramps, I'm home!"

Derek turned toward the doorway, quite unprepared for what was to happen next.

Katy Kruger burst through the front door. Her bright red hair was pulled back in a ponytail and she was wearing a summerweight pink T-shirt and faded jeans. She carried a bag of groceries.

"Gramps, you'll never guess what—" She stopped dead in her tracks and stared at the stranger sitting in the rocking chair. The stranger wasn't a stranger at all. It was Derek Randall, and he was staring back at her with an expression of ludicrous disbelief.

"Katy!" The name practically came out as a croak. *"Katy?"* he repeated in utter astonishment. Had the world turned upside down, or was the enchanting creature who had obsessed his thoughts for the past week actually standing here in front of him? Here, in a tiny country town that he'd never heard of until yesterday.

"Derek!" Katy exclaimed in amazement. "What on earth are you doing here?"

"I should be asking you the same question."

"I *live* here."

Derek shook his head as light dawned. "You mean *you're* the Katy of Baby Katy, the doll?"

"Yes." For some unknown reason, she felt a strange sensation of disappointment. For a moment, Katy had erroneously assumed that Derek Randall had come here, searching for her, for a completely different reason. She didn't even dare tell herself what that reason was.

"I gather that the two of you know each other?" Leo Kruger interrupted with a faint air of surprise.

"Yes, we know each other," Derek declared softly. "Katy, if you only knew how I've been looking for you everywhere."

She looked dubious. "I thought you were here on *business.*"

"I am... that is, I *was*— Oh, just forget that for a moment!" Derek stood up and took several long strides toward her. She was even more lovely than he had remembered, especially with that clinging top and those snug jeans. If her grandfather hadn't been staring curiously at them, he might have taken her in his arms right there and then. "You never told me your last name, and Marvin was no help at all!"

"What *about* Marvin?"

"He's somewhere in the Caribbean, and—"

"Are there sharks in the Caribbean?" Katy interrupted.

"Many."

"Good!" She gave a satisfied smile.

"Anyhow, I couldn't reach Marvin for your last name and address," Derek continued. "I never dreamed for a minute that—"

"Why did you want my address?"

Piercing silver-gray eyes locked with hers. "Why, indeed, Katy?"

For a moment, Katy's knees turned to jelly. Everything she had remembered feeling about this man had not been a product of an overactive imagination. Unlike J.B., this man had the ability to look right into the very core of her being. No, J. B. Halloran and his tentative hand-holding on their movie date had never evoked a reaction like this! Suddenly reality intruded. "How's Lorna?" The words were dragged from her lips.

"I have no idea." Derek's own mouth was taut. "Nor do I care."

Katy fought the lightness that was rising inside her. "Oh, really? I thought you two were an item."

"No, Katy. If you'd only give me a chance to explain what a misunderstanding that all was—"

"It's really not any of my business."

"Oh, I think that it's very much your business." Derek took a step closer, and drew the heavy bag of groceries out of Katy's arms. He set it down on the carpet. "Why don't you let me do the explaining over dinner?"

"Dinner?" she repeated as if she'd never heard of the word.

"Yes, dinner." Derek smiled. Suddenly everything was so bright and clear. He'd never felt so light-hearted before. There was no copyright to acquire. No contract. To hell with everything. Here was Katy. He had found her, completely out of the blue. To Derek Randall, who had never placed much store in luck or mystical signs, it seemed like some kind of omen. Forget Consolidated Industries and his business here. Right now, it didn't seem to matter.

"I . . . I can't have dinner with you, Derek," Katy said slowly.

He quirked an eyebrow. "Why not?"

"Because—" she paused uncomfortably "—I already have a date."

Derek tensed. "You have a date?" This was not something he had foreseen.

"In fact—" Katy appeared uneasy "—I really have to go change now."

Cancel the damn date! Derek wanted to shout at her. But the same barrier that had prevented him from chasing after Katy when she misinterpreted his relationship with Lorna held him back once more. His pride just couldn't allow Derek to lose control. His lips set in a thin line. "Fine," he heard himself reply in a flat unemotional tone. "Perhaps another time, then."

Katy looked at him strangely for a moment. "Does that mean you'll be staying in town?"

"Yes," Derek answered with deliberate coolness. "I have business to conduct. I intend to remain in Green Meadow until it's finished." He extended his hand to Leo Kruger, who shook it in puzzlement. With a curt nod to Katy, he turned and walked out of the house.

"How on earth do you know that man?" Leo Kruger asked his granddaughter for what seemed to be the tenth time.

Katy continued to stare out of the window distractedly. She had been so dumbstruck after seeing Derek Randall that her own reaction had been startling. When he'd asked her out to dinner, every instinct in her body had shouted yes! Wasn't it what she had longed for ever since that evening at the party? Hadn't she fantasized endlessly about meeting the man again and about all the clever things she would say to him? But the truth was, the memory of Lorna kept intruding on the scene. It went to the very heart of all Katy's insecurities. Derek Randall could be a dangerous man in many ways, and one way in particular frightened Katy. It would be so easy for a man like him to make her lose her inhibitions. He was so vital, so very masculine. There was something profoundly disturbing about Derek Randall...something Katy was convinced she would be unable to handle. It all came down to her appalling lack of experience. If she let him into her life, a man with his easy confidence and sophistication, he could hurt her so effortlessly. There was no way Katy could hold her own with the Lornas of this world. Why should she even try?

"Well, it's quite apparent to me," Leo Kruger remarked with vague amusement, "that no matter *how* you happen to know that city boy, he obviously likes you a great deal."

"Who's that, Gramps?" Katy snapped back to reality.

"Who am I talking about, indeed! The Randall fellow, of course."

"I wouldn't go reading a lot into the situation." Katy shrugged.

"Are you kidding? I've never seen any man so happy to see someone in my entire life!" He looked puzzled. "Why did you turn him down, girl? That just isn't like you."

"I already have a date with J.B."

"Oh, really?"

"Yes, *really*." It was the truth. The handsome sheriff had asked her out for dinner and drinks at the one restaurant in Green Meadow. Both had seemed to enjoy each other's easy company during the past week, although nothing of a more romantic nature had occurred than a good-night peck on the cheek. Not yet, anyhow.

"Still, I don't quite understand why you turned Randall down. A fellow like him would be quite a catch."

Katy stared at the elderly man in disbelief. "Gramps! You actually think I would do something so insensitive as to break a date with somebody as nice as J.B.? I don't treat my *friends* that way! Besides, I thought you wanted me to go out with J.B."

"Of course I do!"

"In fact, I thought you were his greatest fan. You've been pushing the two of us together ever since I graduated from high school!"

"Very well, I confess." Leo paused thoughtfully. "Still, certain things are rather difficult to explain. You see, I couldn't help but notice something between the two of you just now. Something I've never seen between you and J.B., as tough as that is for me to admit."

"What something is that?" Katy grew uncomfortable. Could her grandfather actually notice the effect that Derek Randall was having on her? What was more disturbing, was he actually implying that *she* actually had an effect on Derek, as well? It seemed impossible!

Leo gave a frown and thrust his hands into his pockets. "If I have to explain to you what that so-called 'something' is, then you must be the densest female in the entire county!" He shook his head in utter resignation. "Have a good time with J.B., honey.'' Then he picked up the newspaper and turned to the crossword puzzle.

Katy took extra care when she prepared for her date with J.B. She wasn't exactly sure why she found it so important to wear just the right summer dress, and take special pains with her hairstyle. It had never seemed that important before. After all, it was still just 'good old J.B.', wasn't it? Why did she suddenly have an impulse to wear perfume instead of her usual light cologne?

The result was that J.B. Halloran was frankly mystified when he came by to pick her up. He stared at Katy for a moment, his eyes bright blue with both appreciation and bewilderment. ''You, uh, you look very nice tonight, Katy,'' he finally remarked.

''Thanks, J.B.'' She gave him her warmest smile. As usual, J.B. wore a corduroy sport jacket and jeans. When not wearing his official sheriff's uniform, this outfit was as formally as J.B. dressed. In fact, it was said that no human being on the face of the earth had ever seen J.B. wear a suit. It was assumed the man didn't even own one.

There was only one problem involved with dating the sheriff of Green Meadow. In a town where the law enforcement contingent was a total of three, the sheriff was rarely off duty. Going out to a restaurant with a man who carried a walkie-talkie could be somewhat distracting. But then again, this *was* a small town.

Usually nothing much happened here. To be sure, during the summer more people were out and about in Green Meadow. But most of the calls involved stranded motorists, missing cats, or the occasional case of drunk and disorderly conduct outside Whitey's Tavern.

In Green Meadow everyone knew everybody else. In the Green Meadow Restaurant, people all had their favorite tables. When Katy and J.B. walked in, they naturally had to stop by nearly every one of them to say hello. The Torbor twins were there with their father. Tim, Ida and some of the other high school teachers sat at another table. As for the other denizens of the town, they all seemed delighted to see Katy and J.B. together. In most people's minds, Katy and J.B. were already a couple.

Roscoe Schenk, the plump chef and proprietor, rushed over to greet them. "Katy, you're as pretty as a picture!"

"Thanks, Roscoe." She hugged him warmly and sat down in one of the roomy captain's chairs. The sea had a fascination for Roscoe Schenk, so the inside of the restaurant featured nautical motifs. The windows were designed to resemble portholes, and several large sailfish hung on the walls alongside fishnets draped between several battered life preservers from old navy vessels.

"Hey, J.B.," Roscoe exclaimed. "Did you ever find out who stole the hood ornament from Winifred Pym's 1938 Hudson?"

J.B. gave his usual vague smile. "No, Roscoe, but I've issued an all points bulletin on it." He eased himself into the chair opposite Katy and stretched out his long legs into the aisle.

"Are you both having the turkey dinner?" Roscoe inquired. It was just a polite formality. For the past thirty years, Friday night had always been Turkey Special Night at the Green Meadow Restaurant.

"Can I ask you a question?" J.B. inquired as they were served their soup.

"Sure, J.B."

"Is it my imagination, or are you somewhat preoccupied tonight?"

"Uh, what makes you say that?" Katy stammered.

J.B. shrugged. "Just perceptive, I guess." He paused thoughtfully. "You know, it's hasn't escaped my notice that everybody in this room, not to mention this entire town, practically has the two of us walking up the aisle."

Katy practically choked on her clam chowder. "J.B., honestly!"

"Does that bother you?" His gaze was steady.

"To be frank, I hadn't given it much thought." Discussing the matter was a bit embarrassing, but Katy's answer was absolutely sincere. The truth was that she hadn't really considered marriage to J.B. Halloran as a likely prospect.

"Oh, you haven't?" J.B. sounded more surprised than disappointed. Like most handsome men, he possessed a healthy ego.

Katy put down her soup spoon, reached across the table and affectionately grasped his hand. "C'mon, J.B., what is this all about?"

"I think you know." His own fingers tightened on Katy's.

She studied his expression for a long moment. "J.B., I know you like me, and we have a good time together." There was a pause. "But you aren't in love with me."

"One of these days I *could* be," J.B. argued. "In fact, I might be halfway in love with you already, Katy."

"But you aren't." She shook her head insistently. "Be honest, J.B. You know you aren't. You're still waiting for the right girl to come along."

The faraway expression was back on the young sheriff's face once more. "Maybe the things we wait for don't really exist except in our fantasies."

"When you stop talking like that, J.B., then you'll know you're in love."

His sigh was a heavy one. "How did you get to be so old and wise, anyhow?"

"I'm not, J.B.," she replied softly. "It's just that you and I are very much alike."

He gave an uncharacteristic chuckle. "Let's make a deal, Katy. Ten years from now, if we're both still single, let's say 'the hell with it' and get married anyhow!"

"You've got a deal, J.B.!"

They were still laughing when a newcomer entered the dining room. Derek Randall was being shown to a nearby table by Roscoe, when his hard silver eyes caught the sight of Katy and that tow-headed police officer. They were laughing and holding hands. For the first time in his life, blind jealous fury boiled up inside Derek. So this was the man Katy was dating.

On his home turf, Derek felt he could compete with anyone. In the city, a man didn't have to be handsome to sweep a woman off her feet. Success and power had an allure all their own. Derek was sure that his monthly salary alone was more than this rural policeman earned in an entire year. But Green Meadow was *this* man's turf. It was probably prestigious to be dating the local lawman. But damn, did the guy have to be so good-looking? He was practically a dead ringer for Robert Redford. How on earth was he supposed to compete with *that*? Derek had never felt so utterly deflated.

And then Katy looked up in his direction and froze. Since Derek had to pass her table to arrive at his own, he found himself pausing for a moment in front of her, unable to stop himself.

"Hello, Katy," he said quietly.

Self-conscious, she let go of J.B.'s hand. "Oh, hi, Derek."

There was an awkward pause. J.B. studied the obvious tension between the two of them for a moment, then asked, "Do the two of you know each other?"

Derek ignored him. "So, this was the date you didn't want to break?"

"That's right," Katy retorted.

"I see." Derek's voice was icy.

J.B. scratched his chin. "Mr. Randall, did you actually ask her to break our date?"

Katy looked at J.B. curiously. "And how do *you* know him?"

"I didn't give Mr. Randall a speeding ticket this afternoon." He hesitated. "Maybe I *should* have," he said wryly, "seeing as he tried to sabotage our date tonight."

"It's very unlike you not to give out a speeding ticket, J.B.," Katy observed, feeling she had to say *something*.

"True enough, honey, but after all, it is the man's birthday."

Derek felt another hot ember of jealousy in the pit of his stomach. Just hearing J.B. refer to Katy as *honey* was almost more than he could take, right at this moment.

"Oh." Katy's expression softened involuntarily. "It's your birthday today, Derek?"

To Derek, who had been quite unprepared for the sudden warmth in her voice, the effect was immediate. A slow smile spread across his face. "Yes, Katy. It's my birthday." As a rule he had little use for birthdays. During his childhood, they had always been disappointing footnotes to unhappy years. They had never been occasions his parents remembered to celebrate. But if the fact that today happened to mark another anniversary of his birth was enough to bring that sweet expression back to Katy's face... well, then, birthdays *did* have their uses, after all. And he intended to milk the situation for everything it was worth.

Katy had never felt so rotten in her life! Here was Derek Randall, alone in a strange town on his birthday! Of course he had asked her to have dinner with him! Whoever wanted to spend his birthday alone in a restaurant? Whatever had possessed her to be so rude to the man? So very insensitive? "I'm sorry, Derek," she murmured gently. "I had no idea it was your birthday."

"That's all right, Katy. I really don't mind."

She turned to J.B. "He's got to have a cake. It wouldn't be a birthday without a cake."

J.B. twisted his lips and gazed up at the ceiling. "By all means, Katy. Let's make sure the man gets his birthday cake."

Derek waved a hand. "Oh, please, don't bother. After all, it's the *thought* that counts."

The sheriff glanced knowingly at Derek. "You can just bet that I'm quite aware of what exactly the thought is, Mr. Randall."

"Oh, please—" he extended his hand politely "—call me Derek."

"Then I suppose you'd better call me J.B.," the other man conceded. He gestured for Roscoe.

The restaurant owner anxiously rushed over to the table. "Is everything okay, J.B.?"

"Just fine. Derek, this is Roscoe." J.B. paused resignedly. "Derek will be joining us for dinner, Roscoe. And it's his birthday."

"His birthday?" Roscoe's eyes lighted up. "Then I'd better go and prepare the cake!" Without another word, the jovial restaurateur bounded off to the kitchen.

"Please, pull up a chair, Derek," J.B. murmured.

Derek studied the other man for a long moment. He was usually a rather shrewd judge of character, but this country sheriff was a difficult person to read. Just how involved were Katy and J.B.? He couldn't imagine someone allowing another man to muscle in on his date. The whole situation was hard to figure, but then, who was he to look a gift horse in the mouth? Derek wanted to spend time with Katy, and if this was the second time in a row that one of her dates was stupid enough to let him have a chance...well, all the better.

"Thanks," Derek replied finally. "I believe I will." He pulled a chair from an adjoining table and drew it along the side at the aisle, right between Katy and J.B.

"Tonight might be your birthday, Derek," J.B. said with faint amusement, "but tomorrow, if I were you, I'd be very careful about obeying all our traffic laws."

Katy couldn't tell if J.B. was joking or not. The truth was, she'd never been in a situation like this before. In New York City, she and her friends had constantly bemoaned the horrible shortage of men. And now, quite unexpectedly, here she was with not one but *two* males, who both wanted to spend time with her. It was quite an ego boost.

"Don't worry, J.B.," Derek was saying. "You can bet I'll be extremely careful in the future." But as he said this, he was staring at Katy, who seemed at a loss for words.

J. B. Halloran, having nothing better to do, gazed up at the ceiling for the second time. And just then there was a squawk from his walkie-talkie. Almost with relief, he pressed the button down. "Go ahead, Harry," he murmured.

Everyone in the restaurant strained their ears to listen as a scratchy voice on the other end mumbled some message about an altercation at Whitey's Tavern.

"I'll be right over," J.B. muttered, and replaced the walkie-talkie in his belt.

"The Taylor brothers again?" Katy asked.

J.B. shrugged. "It only happens once a month. I suppose we should be grateful for that." He pushed back his chair from the table and stood up. "Sorry about this, Katy, but I'll have to go." He glanced over at Derek. "I'm sure I can count on you to look after her for me."

"You can bet on it." Derek nodded with scarcely concealed triumph. Things were proceeding very well, indeed!

As J.B. pulled his massive frame away from the table and past Derek, he leaned over and said in a low voice. "By the way, birthday boy, I think it's only fair that *you* pick up the check." Unexpectedly he broke into a broad smile. With a wave to Katy, J.B. strode out of the restaurant.

"Alone at last," Derek murmured under his breath.

"What did you say?" Katy was flustered. In the company of J.B., she felt she could handle Derek Randall. But now the two of them were alone....

"It looks like we're having dinner together, after all," he said, his voice silky.

Katy could only look at him. Strange. She had forgotten how devastatingly attractive he was. He was still wearing the perfectly cut charcoal suit he had worn earlier in the day, but had changed from a white shirt to a plain yellow one. The color accentuated the tan on Derek's rugged face and the silvery tint of his eyes. The jagged scar running from his jawline halfway up his cheek still puzzled her. She longed to ask him how and where he'd received that scar, but it seemed too intrusive a question to ask right now. Especially on a person's birthday. A part of Katy wanted to reach out to Derek in sympathy for whatever unfortunate circumstance had caused that injury. She'd never wanted to care for a man this way before.

"Do you have any idea how badly I wanted to see you again, Katy?" There was a strange urgency in Derek's tone. He reached out and took her fingers in his firm grasp.

Holding J.B.'s hand, as she had done only a few minutes before, had evoked none of the tingly sensations that Katy was experiencing from Derek's touch. It was especially odd, because J.B.'s grip was every bit as firm and warm as this man's. And yet something had been missing from J.B.'s touch . . . something elusive and hard to define. But in Derek's grasp, here it was. And whatever it was, it made Katy continue to tingle. "I don't understand. . . ." She was stammering. What was this man doing to her? How could he reduce her to a mass of quivering jelly just with the touch of a hand? This was ridiculous! She wasn't some anemic heroine in a Victorian novel who swooned every time a handsome man drew near. No, Katy corrected herself again, not *every* time a man touched her hand. Just *this* time. Just *this* man.

Meanwhile, Derek was determined not to let anything come between the two of them again. It was crucial to clear up the misunderstanding about Lorna before it caused any more problems. "About that night at the party," he began, still keeping her hand tightly in his own. "You never did let me explain about Lorna."

Involuntarily, Katy wanted to pull away. "It really isn't any of my business."

The man sitting so close to her shook his head assertively. "No, it is your business. I want it to be your business, Katy." He drew a deep breath. Talking about himself did not come easily to Derek, but it seemed important to explain to the young woman next to him what had happened. "Lorna and I went out for several months. We both moved in the same business circles and had the same friends. It was what you might call convenient."

Katy shifted uncomfortably in her seat. She really didn't want to hear any of this. It was actually quite painful to picture Derek and the beautiful Lorna together, dancing, kissing... making love.

He seemed to know what she was thinking without her saying a word. "Listen to me, Katy. Whatever Lorna and I shared together, it was over weeks ago." The raw sincerity in his tone was unmistakable. "There were never any deep feelings involved on either part, no matter what Lorna's behavior led you to believe." Derek waited. He had swallowed his pride this way because he wanted Katy badly, but at a certain point she just had to meet him halfway. It was crucial for her to believe what he was now telling her. It meant everything that this lovely creature should like him enough to *want* to believe him. To take his words on trust.

Katy slowly raised her green eyes to his. "I believe you, Derek," she murmured. "It was wrong of me to jump to conclusions."

"Are we friends, then?" he asked beguilingly.

"Yes, we're friends." Of course, they were friends, she thought. Wasn't that what she had wanted all along?

Dinner proved to be a highly pleasant affair. After thick slices of turkey with dressing and mashed potatoes, Roscoe brought out a traditional layer cake decorated with icing rosettes and a score of birthday candles. "I wasn't sure how many to put on," he declared after the entire room had lustily joined in a chorus of "Happy Birthday to You."

Derek glanced at what seemed to be at least forty candles blazing on top of the cake, and gave a helpless laugh. Then, to applause, he blew out all the candles in one great puff of breath.

"Congratulations," Katy said and smiled, her hands folded quite still in her lap.

Derek quirked an eyebrow thoughtfully. "I don't know about this, Katy."

"About what?" She was puzzled.

"In a town that makes such a big fuss about birthdays—what with no speeding tickets issued by the local police, and birthday cakes appearing like magic in restaurants—it just seems odd you would neglect to observe traditional birthday etiquette...."

"I don't understand—"

He tried to look casual. "Aren't I supposed to get a birthday kiss, or something?"

Katy turned the faintest shade of pink. "Oh!" was all she could reply.

Derek couldn't believe that she was actually blushing. "Am I embarrassing you, Katy?"

"Yes." Here was Derek Randall asking her to kiss him, for heaven's sake!

His mouth curved up in a gentle smile. "I don't mean to embarrass you, but it *is* my birthday, after all." Besides, when would he have a better excuse? Derek tilted his head and pointed to one rough cheek. "Here I am, alone in a strange town on my birthday. Doesn't a man deserve even one congratulatory peck on the cheek from a single compassionate soul?"

Unable to resist such an entreaty, Katy leaned over and briefly touched her lips to his face in a feather-light kiss. He smelled of soap and spicy after-shave. Although the gesture lasted no more than a second or so, her pulse began to race uncontrollably. She pulled back. "Was that what you meant?" Katy somehow managed to find her voice.

There was an odd glitter in Derek's eyes. "Yes, that was just what I meant."

Chapter Five

That brief kiss on the cheek had not passed unnoticed by the other diners at the Green Meadow Restaurant, and Katy knew it was a foregone conclusion that the innocent little gesture would be the subject of conversation over many a cup of coffee the next morning. Katy Kruger did not usually kiss strange men from New York City in the middle of a crowded restaurant. Certainly not the Katy Kruger *they* knew. And what about poor J.B.? The stunned but envious glances from the Torbor twins and an exasperated glare from Ida Johnson gave Katy a pretty accurate assessment of what she could expect. None of these reactions had gone unnoticed by Derek Randall.

"What was that all about?" he asked as they walked out into the parking lot.

"Nothing," Katy said quickly.

"I believe it *was* something," came the quiet reply.

She sighed. "All right. If you must know, being that this is such a small town, everybody in the restaurant was, well, kind of surprised to see me kiss you, no matter how innocent the reason. They believe that J.B. and I—"

Derek stopped dead in his tracks. He seemed suddenly an ominous figure against the night sky, the moonlight illuminating his hard features. "What *about* you and J.B.?"

Katy gave a sigh. "Do we have to talk about this now? It's getting late—"

"Damn *right* we have to talk about it now." Derek's voice was tense. "What is that man to you, Katy?"

"We're friends," she said and gazed up at him in puzzlement. Why did he sound so angry?

"Just *friends*?"

"Can I help it if everybody in town thinks we're halfway down the aisle already?"

There was a strained expression on Derek's taut face. "Why do they think that, Katy?"

She folded her arms stubbornly. "I don't want to discuss it."

"Oh, but it was perfectly all right to discuss *my* relationship with Lorna!" His words practically came out as a sneer.

"You're the one who brought up Lorna, not me," she reminded him. "Anyhow, that was different."

Derek crossed his arms and stared down at her in the dim light. "What's so different about it, Katy?"

She was at a complete loss right then. How could Katy explain that her relationship with J.B. had none of the intimacy and sophistication that clearly characterized his affair with Lorna? It was something so personal that she was unable to put it into words. She had no idea that Derek Randall would misinterpret her silence.

"Fine!" he uttered harshly. "Don't explain. It obviously isn't necessary." With a hasty stride he reached his car and angrily unlocked the passenger door.

His anger bewildered her, but she didn't say anything. Katy quietly slid into the passenger seat and waited for him to shut the door.

The silence on the ride home was so uncomfortable that Katy felt she had to finally speak up. She searched for a subject that had nothing to do with Lorna, J.B. or relationships in general, then cleared her throat. "Thank you for dinner. It was very nice."

Derek kept his eyes on the road. "You're welcome."

More silence. She sighed and tried again. "Do you realize that you're the only person who ever locked a car in Green Meadow?"

Instead of evoking a chuckle, this remark seemed to almost irritate Derek. "Really?"

He was thinking that he didn't give a damn whether people in Green Meadow locked their cars or not. Everything that was considered whimsical and charming about this isolated little town suddenly annoyed him in the extreme. It was all a lot of country corn. Until a few minutes ago, he had been so sure about Katy's attraction to him. He'd been so confident in his own ability to come right in and sweep the girl off her feet. But her reaction when he'd brought up the subject of J. B. Halloran had stunned him. She'd been so defensive, and Derek's instincts told him that Katy was hiding something. He replayed in his mind the sheriff's casual attitude at the restaurant. Up to that point, Derek had misinterpreted his lack of possessiveness for something else. Now, too late, he realized the man had been acting that way out of confidence. Derek gripped the steering wheel tightly. J. B. Halloran was so confident in his relationship with Katy that he could afford to be magnanimous. Damn! Whatever made Derek think he stood a chance with Katy Kruger, anyhow? She was no Lorna, impressed with his wealth and status. Katy might have resembled an elegant socialite on that first night in her dazzling sequined evening dress, but now it was apparent that in her hometown, at least, she played by a different set of rules. Up here in rustic Green Meadow, Derek Randall simply didn't have a chance against the towering, handsome J. B. Halloran. He'd been a fool to even try.

A cold wave of realization washed over him. For the past week he'd been acting like a moron. Obsessed with a woman he barely even knew. It was time to stop this lunacy and behave like a normal human being again. He was Derek Randall, the boy wonder of Consolidated Industries. He had always placed his career ahead of everything else, and it had paid off. Morgan Strickland was grooming him to step into the presidency of Consolidated upon his retirement. Derek pressed his lips together tightly. In the past seven days he'd neglected his work, behaving instead like some lovesick schoolboy. Well, the woman obviously preferred another man. That was *that*. Face reality. Accept defeat and move on, he told himself angrily. He'd been lost on a ridiculous romantic tangent. He should have known *that* kind of happiness was never meant for him. Derek faced the painful fact that he should stick to the one thing he knew best—business. That's why he was here in the first place, wasn't it? *Business*.

Abruptly he pulled the car to the side of the dark, winding road, and cleared his throat. "Let's talk, Katy."

She stared at him in the moonlight, and felt a sudden chill on the bare skin of her arms. Why had he stopped the car?

"Talk about what?" Her voice was tremulous.

"Business."

She quirked an eyebrow. "Now? You want to talk about business *now*?"

His tone was almost sarcastic. "What else would you suggest we talk about?" He mistook Katy's odd silence for assent, and continued. "I presume your grandfather has discussed Consolidated Industries' extremely generous offer with you."

"No." What on earth was he talking about? Katy's bewilderment temporarily overrode her sense of disappointment. What kind of business could Derek have to discuss with *her*?

"You own the rights to the Baby Katy doll, and we want those rights."

This revelation was more confusing to Katy than the astonishing change in Derek's tone. Why had he become so cold and aloof all of a sudden? Or—Katy's heart fell—had he wanted to discuss business all along? She'd been so surprised to see Derek Randall standing in her living room this afternoon that she hadn't really questioned what had brought him there. Gramps had merely mentioned that the man was an executive vice president at Consolidated, the corporation that had contracted with the Kruger factory to handle some of its small plastic production. He had neglected to tell her anything else, and now Katy wondered why. "You want the rights?" she said slowly. "For what reason?"

Derek twisted his lips. "It's not *my* idea. If you want to know the truth, I'm dead-set against it. But the marketing geniuses are convinced a reissued Baby Katy will be the hit of next Christmas season."

She was staggered. "Your company wants to put the doll into production again?"

"If you agree to sign over the copyright, I'm authorized to hand you a banker's draft for one million dollars." There was something hollow in Derek's tone.

"One million dollars?" She practically gasped.

"Or if you prefer, a percentage of the profits." Derek eyed her steadily. "I'd advise against that, however, because it's my opinion that the profits won't be worth mentioning."

"What do you mean?"

He shifted his lanky frame in the roomy car seat, and turned to face her. "I don't consider the doll to be a wise investment. I think the venture will be a bust." He was back to sounding like his old self again, cool and analytical. "I'd advise you to take the money up front." Derek tried to ignore the luminous green of her eyes, but even in the dim light he was bewitched by the color.

"Why," Katy asked slowly, "don't you consider it a wise investment?"

"I already told you." Derek struggled to remain aloof. "The venture can't possibly succeed."

"What makes you so...so confident? Do you dislike the doll so much?" She tried not to sound hurt.

"There's nothing personal about this, Katy, although I *do* happen to find all toys a foolish, self-indulgent waste of time."

To the granddaughter of Leo Kruger, Derek Randall's words were tantamount to sacrilege. "You don't like toys...at all?"

"Not particularly."

"I'm sure, though, when you were a child—"

"I'm not a child *now*," he uttered deprecatingly. "As you might recall, I have just celebrated my birthday."

"Yes, but as a little boy, you must have liked toys. What child doesn't have a favorite car or teddy bear?"

His jaw tightened. "If you want my opinion, I happen to find the crass commercialization of the toy industry does children a great disservice. Toys do more harm than good, and the sooner youngsters are made to face reality instead of a fantasy world, the better."

Once again, she caught a glimpse of that same vulnerability so briefly revealed the night of the penthouse party, when she had made that careless comment about his looks. Katy was perceptive enough to sense that the man was holding something back.

He cleared his throat again. The last thing Derek cared to discuss right now was his philosophy on toys or his own rotten childhood. "One million dollars is a great deal of money, Katy. Think what it could mean to you."

Katy paused. For the past few moments she had been so busy thinking about Derek, trying to figure out some vital clue to what made the man tick that she had quite forgotten about Consolidated's staggering offer. One million dollars! Derek was right. What wonderful things it might mean for her and her grandfather! For the Kruger factory. Excitement coursed through her—for the entire town of Green Meadow. To see the factory alive again, making *toys* as it was meant to do. How wonderful that would be! "You're right." She looked at him hopefully. "It could mean everything."

Derek sat there, watching the way the moonlight glimmered on her hair and the bare skin of her shoulders. He was trying desperately to remain unmoved. Every impulse in him cried out to pull Katy into his arms and feel the softness of her body against his own. The touch of her lips on his cheek had been exquisite torture. It had left Derek wanting more, so much more. He had to fight to remind himself that Katy's obvious preference was for muscular blond lawmen who looked like film stars.

Hastily Derek started up the engine and thrust the rental car back into gear. "It's been a long day for me, Katy. Why don't we discuss this further over breakfast?"

"Yes...of course." Katy nodded tentatively, somewhat baffled at such an abrupt end to the conversation. She studied her companion's sharply etched profile as he concentrated on the road ahead. "I'll need time to think it over," she added.

Derek gave a brusque nod. "Yes, by all means."

Not another word was spoken until the beige Buick pulled into the long driveway of the Kruger home. Except for a single light over the front porch, the pink Victorian house was in total darkness. Leo Kruger kept early hours.

"Where are you staying?" Katy inquired politely, knowing all along there was only one possible answer: the Mother Goose Motel and Cottages.

Derek knew she was only making conversation and smiled thinly. "Your local five-star resort. I believe all the cabins are named for various characters in classic literature. I'm in Number Four, the Jack Sprat cabin."

She couldn't help grinning to herself. The last word anyone might use to describe the Mother Goose Motel was "resort." The burly proprietors, Tiny Taylor and his brother Edgar, hadn't purchased new linen for the lumpy mattresses in twenty years, and the mismatched towels in the bathrooms had more holes than a golf course.

"Will you be staying in Green Meadow long?" she suddenly blurted.

There was an odd light in his eyes. "Why?" he murmured. "Does that really make a difference, or are you just asking to be polite?"

"I . . . I wanted to know, Derek."

Derek. Just hearing her say his name in that soft, breathy tone was wreaking havoc on his senses. There was an odd constriction in his throat. How long was he staying? He'd like to stay long enough to make Katy forget that Sheriff J. B. Halloran ever existed. Aloud, however, he merely replied, "Until I finish this business for Consolidated and get you to sign on the dotted line, Katy."

"Oh."

For a moment, Derek imagined that he detected a trace of disappointment in her voice, but decided it was just wishful thinking on his part. "When is a convenient time for you tomorrow?"

Those luminous green eyes were still turned toward him. "I'm flexible."

"About nine o'clock?"

"Fine."

"They *do* serve breakfast at the Green Meadow Restaurant, don't they?"

Katy continued to study his gaunt features. "I have a better idea. Why don't you come over *here* for breakfast instead?"

Derek paused. "All right."

"Do you like blueberry pancakes?"

The hardness in his face began to melt immediately. "Yes, Katy. I like them very much."

"Good. As it happens I make the best ones in town." In truth, it was the only thing Katy knew how to cook that wasn't a total disaster. But she certainly wasn't going to let Derek know *that*. "It's an old recipe of my grandmother's. The blueberries grow wild in the backyard."

"How interesting." Derek watched the play of the moonlight on her hair again. There were few things more subtly sensual to a man than the simple act of a woman preparing a meal especially for him, he reflected.

Katy was suddenly nervous. "Did I thank you for dinner?"

"Yes." Against his volition, Derek found himself leaning forward to brush a silky strand of hair away from her eye.

The unexpected gesture gave Katy goose bumps. "I'll see you at nine, then," she blurted quickly.

"I'll look forward to it," Derek remarked quietly, wondering how he could get away with kissing Katy good-night. A most unusual problem for Derek Randall. Never in the past could he ever recall hesitating about something so simple as a good-night kiss. Before, if he had the impulse to kiss a woman, he just acted upon it. But with Katy Kruger, he felt as if he was back in grade school again. What if she pulled away from him? However badly he wanted the softness of her mouth at this moment, his ego just couldn't take any more battering tonight.

"Well," she said in that wonderful breathy voice that had the most disconcerting effect on him. "Good night, Derek." Before he could react, she opened the passenger door and quickly stepped out of the car.

"Katy, wait!" Derek thrust open his own door and bounded out after her. "At least let me be a gentleman and walk you up the steps." As soon as the words were out of his mouth, Derek felt like some character in a corny play.

But Katy merely nodded and said, "All right." She was desperately hoping he couldn't hear her heart hammering in her ears.

Derek was matching her step for step up toward the gingerbread-trimmed front porch, when she suddenly lost her footing and stumbled. "Oh—"

In the next instant, Katy felt herself caught up in a pair of powerful arms and Derek's hard body pressed against the softness of her own.

"Are you all right?" His voice came out a rasp.

"Yes, thank you!" she responded just a bit too breathlessly. In all her twenty-four years of climbing up these same steps, Katy had never once tripped. It was the strangest thing, she wanted to say, but at this moment all she could think of was how delicious it felt to be held by Derek in this startlingly intimate way. The goose bumps came back again.

"You're very welcome," Derek murmured against her ear, astonished by the intensity of his own arousal. He didn't want to let go of Katy, not yet, anyhow. She felt too damn good. And her faint flowery perfume went right to his head. He looked down into those glowing green eyes and was nearly done for. Fighting every impulse to kiss the breath out of Katy Kruger, Derek put her firmly from him. "You ought to be more careful on these stairs," he said, forcing his voice to sound normal.

"That's never happened before," Katy answered shakily.

"There's always a first time." Derek felt some kind of reply was required from him. "I'll see you in the morning, Katy," he added with deliberate blandness. Then he turned, walked briskly down the steps and back to his car. And drove off into the night.

Chapter Six

Leo Kruger had very strong reasons for not having told his granddaughter about Consolidated Industries' bid for the Katy doll. First of all, he wanted the girl to make up her own mind. His own opinion on the subject was quite definite. He didn't want anyone or any corporation fooling around with one of *his* creations. He'd fought that for years, and succeeded, until now. But secondly, it had occurred to him that his motives might be selfish ones. Perhaps it was wrong of him to resist selling out. After all, it was just one of many dolls. What good did it do to be proud and independent, if it meant that the people he loved had to suffer for it? One million dollars, as Derek Randall had so accurately pointed out, was quite a

```
************************************************************
*  You may have already won a lifetime of cash payments *
*  totaling up to $1,000,000.00!  Play our Sweepstakes  *
*  Game--Here's how it works...                         *
************************************************************
```

Each of the first three tickets has a unique Sweepstakes number.
If your Sweepstakes numbers match any of the winning numbers
selected by our computer, you could win the amount shown under
the gold rub-off on that ticket.

Using an eraser, rub off the gold boxes on tickets #1-3 to
reveal how much each ticket could be worth if it is a winning
ticket. You must return the <u>entire</u> card to be eligible. (See
official rules in the back of this book for details.)

At the same time you play your tickets for big cash prizes,
Silhouette also invites you to participate in a special trial of
our Reader Service by accepting one or more FREE book(s) from
Silhouette Romance.™ To request your free book(s), just rub off
the gold box on ticket #4 to reveal how many free book(s) you
will receive.

When you receive your free book(s), we hope you'll enjoy them
and want to see more. So unless we hear from you, every month
we'll send you 6 additional Silhouette Romance™ novels. Each
book is yours to keep for only $2.25* each. There are <u>no</u>
additional charges for shipping and handling and of course, you
may cancel Reader Service privileges at any time by marking
"cancel" on your shipping statement or returning an unopened
shipment of books to us at our expense. Either way your
shipments will stop. You'll receive no more books; you'll have
no further obligation.

PLUS-you get a FREE MYSTERY GIFT!

If you return your game card with <u>**all four gold boxes**</u> rubbed
off, you will also receive a FREE Mystery Gift. It's your
<u>**immediate reward**</u> for sampling your free book(s), <u>**and**</u> it's your
to keep no matter what you decide.

P.S.

Remember, the first set of one or more book(s) is FREE. So ru
off the gold box on ticket #4 and return the entire sheet of
tickets today!

*Terms and prices subject to change without notice.
 Sales taxes applicable in New York and Iowa.

"GIVE YOUR HEART TO SILHOUETTE" SWEEPSTAKES

#1 $1,000,000.00

Rub off to reveal potential value if this is a winning ticket: ▶

$35,000

UNIQUE SWEEPSTAKES NUMBER: 6A 412480

#2 $1,000,000.00

Rub off to reveal potential value if this is a winning ticket: ▶

$10,000

UNIQUE SWEEPSTAKES NUMBER: 7A 414465

#3 $1,000,000.00

Rub off to reveal potential value if this is a winning ticket: ▶

$1,000,000

UNIQUE SWEEPSTAKES NUMBER: 8A 412131

#4 ONE OR MORE FREE BOOKS

HOW MANY FREE BOOKS?
Rub off to reveal number of free books you will receive ▶

4

1672765559

Yes! Enter my sweepstakes numbers in the Sweepstakes and let me know if I've won a cash prize. If gold box on ticket **#4** is rubbed off, I will also receive one or more Silhouette Romance novels as a FREE tryout of the Reader Service, along with a FREE Mystery Gift as explained on the opposite page.

215 CIS HAX8

NAME

ADDRESS   APT.

CITY   STATE   ZIP CODE

DON'T FORGET...

... Return this card today with ticket #4 rubbed off, and receive 4 free books and a free mystery gift.

... You will receive books well before they're available in stores.

... No obligation to buy. You can cancel at any time by writing "cancel" on your statement or returning an unopened shipment to us at our cost.

If offer card is missing, write to: Silhouette Reader Service, 901 Fuhrmann Blvd., P.O. Box 1867, Buffalo, N.Y. 14269-1867 generous offer. It would make life a great deal easier for Katy. He'd hated to see her struggle this past year to support herself through art school. He knew all about the extra jobs and long, hard hours.

So, if some megacorporation wanted to take his wonderfully crafted toy and mass-produce some cheap version of it in one of its overseas factories, why should Leo Kruger protest too loudly? What was more important, a product or a person? Where were his priorities? Wasn't his first and foremost obligation to his own flesh and blood, not to an inanimate object? Yesterday he'd let his temper get the better of him. Halfway through his tirade against Derek Randall, it had occurred to him that the young executive might be right. It would mean a lot for Katy to be well looked after. One million dollars would certainly insure that. What better legacy could he leave his only grandchild? The best thing Leo Kruger knew he could do was to keep his nose out of it. Allow Katy to come to her own conclusions. For that reason, at five o'clock in the morning, the elderly toy maker left to go fishing up at Silverwood Lake with his old high school buddy, Whitey Wilson, the pint-sized owner of Whitey's Tavern.

Katy understood immediately the reason for her grandfather's absence the next morning. It didn't take much to figure out that he wanted her to make up her own mind about giving up the copyright. Actually, she had never been as sentimental about the Baby Katy doll as the other members of the Kruger family. To be honest, mention of the toy brought back some unhappy memories. When Katy was between three and seven, the doll had been at the height of its popularity. Those four years had also been the only unhappy time of Katy's young life. It was then that she had lost her mother and her father. Meanwhile, in school, she was endlessly teased about the doll that bore her name. No one ever seemed to call her simply Katy. She was known as Baby Katy. It was really irritating to a young child. She had, in fact, a deeper attachment to some of her grandfather's other creations, such as the wind-up cars and trucks. Not that she'd ever admit it to the old man; he'd probably be devastated.

During the night, she'd had more time to consider Derek's offer. It was actually quite tempting. But she would have to find out more about what it entailed.

If Katy was completely honest with herself, she'd tossed and turned all through the wee hours more because of Derek Randall than of his business proposition. When she'd slipped on the stairs and he had caught her against his hard strength, it had been shattering. For one breathless instant, it had seemed as if Derek were about to kiss her.

All through her shower that morning, while she took extra pains with her make-up and brushed her shoulder-length hair till it shone, Katy wondered what it would be like to be kissed by Derek Randall. To feel those hard lips on her own. She shivered, but it was a delicious kind of shiver. She had never met anyone as devastatingly masculine as Derek Randall. Katy wished she had the allure of Lorna. She wished she owned some sexy designer outfits, instead of her old print summer dresses and faded jeans. And most of all, Katy wished she knew what Derek Randall really thought about her. It was puzzling, the way the man seemed to burn hot and then cold. One moment she was convinced that he liked her. The next moment he would pull away and be all business. With Katy's lamentably limited amount of experience with men, it was difficult to understand just exactly *what* Derek actually wanted. But there was a nagging fear in the back of her mind that no matter what the man's intentions were, he was still too intimidating. Derek Randall might be both disarmingly vulnerable and overwhelmingly male, but the fact remained that he was also a big-city playboy. And that was more than Katy could possibly handle.

Derek showed up for their breakfast meeting in shirt-sleeves and a tie. His silver eyes lingered on Katy's slender form in those wonderful jeans and clinging blue T-shirt. Every time he saw her, Derek realized he had forgotten how lovely Katy was. But he had come that morning prepared to conduct business in a cool, efficient manner. Then it occurred to him that Leo Kruger was nowhere to be seen. Surely the old man intended to oversee the meeting, the way any inventor with a stake in this business would.

"Where's your grandfather?" he asked curiously, assuming that the man was merely upstairs getting dressed or out buying a newspaper.

Katy tried to sound casual. "He's not here."

"What do you mean, he's not here?"

She shrugged. "He's gone fishing up at the lake."

"Gone fishing?" Derek had an odd note in his voice.

"Oh," Katy said uncomfortably. "I didn't realize you were expecting him to be here."

"Naturally I assumed he'd want to advise you—"

She smiled cryptically. "So did I, Derek. But he was gone before I even woke up. I guess Gramps wants me to make my own decision, without pressure." She thrust her hands into her pockets. "Would you like some orange juice before I serve the coffee?"

Blindly Derek nodded and followed Katy into the huge, sunny kitchen, where stained glass flowers bordered all the beveled windows. Any other time, he would have appreciated the whimsical charm of the hand-painted cabinets and bright wooden chairs, but all he could think of was that the two of them were alone together in this big old house. *Alone.* It made him feel almost reckless. Anything could happen, Derek thought wildly. All thoughts of conducting business and behaving in his usual cool, efficient manner flew right out the window. How could he concentrate on business, knowing that Leo Kruger was miles away and would remain so for the rest of the day? He and Katy were completely alone. Even if it took hours and hours to go over the contracts, the two of them would still be *alone*. Anything could happen, couldn't it?

Katy was completely unaware of Derek's inner turmoil. She had problems of her own to consider. The two of them were all alone. *Anything* could happen.

At first, everything went smoothly. The pancakes were light and just the right shade of golden brown. The conversation was pleasant, and the mood very laid-back. It seemed as if both of them were making a special effort to reduce any tensions that might have been in the air. But in truth, Derek was unable to keep his eyes off Katy. He wondered how she felt when J. B. Halloran put his arms around her slender waist and kissed her. He wondered if she trembled at his touch when the caresses became more intimate. Worst of all, he wondered what Katy's eyes looked like when they made love. It gave him the sharpest pain in his gut to think of another man touching Katy and sharing her most intimate secrets. He couldn't bear the thought of any other man making love to Katy.

Abruptly Derek forced these disturbing images from his mind. He was here on *business*, he reminded himself for the seven-hundredth time. Derek reached for his leather briefcase and pulled a thick sheaf of paper from one of the compartments. "Why don't we look these documents over?" he suggested crisply.

Katy set down her coffee cup. "All right, Derek," she replied in a subdued tone. Did the man have to look so incredibly attractive this morning? With the sleeves of his expensive dress shirt rolled almost up to the elbows, she could see the muscular strength of his forearms. And did he have to sit across the table at just the right angle for her to notice the healthy sheen of his short, brown hair? He was holding out a stack of papers and trying to explain their meaning, but all Katy could think of was how pleasurable the low timbre of his voice sounded to her ears.

"And this clause states that all production of the doll will be completely under the supervision of Consolidated, as well as all advertising and promotional approval."

Katy stopped her reverie and sat up sharply. "What do you mean, 'the production will be completely under Consolidated's supervision'?"

"Just what it says."

"But I thought—"

He looked at her curiously. "You thought *what*?" There was a troubled furrow on her usually smooth forehead. "Does this mean that your corporation has no intention to include my grandfather's factory in any aspect of the doll's production?"

Derek gave a nod. "I thought you understood that from the start."

"No, I didn't," she replied. "You see, I assumed at least *some* of the production line work would take place in Green Meadow. Since your company wanted to use the original molds, it only made sense to me that they'd want to make use of some of the original technicians, as well. You'd be hard-pressed to find workers with their level of skill anywhere, Derek...and the people who hand-sew all the little outfits, you've never seen such perfection—"

"Katy—" Derek shook his head "—I don't mean to burst your bubble, but the kind of work you're talking about is the very reason your grandfather's factory almost went bankrupt. For a company to be successful, it has to look at the bottom line."

"What bottom line?"

Slowly he set down the paper he had been reading aloud to her. "Katy—" his tone was more gentle now "—a multinational corporation like Consolidated is interested in profitability first, and quality second. It can't afford to be sentimental."

"In other words, you're not actually going to reissue the original Baby Katy, but a cheap imitation."

"Yes," Derek answered bluntly, "that's about the size of it." His silvery gaze followed Katy as she stood up from the table and walked over to the window as if in need of fresh air. There was a long silence.

"What you're telling me—" she stared out of the window and into the garden with its cheerful profusion of summer blooms "—is that the workers at the

Kruger factory don't get anything out of this proposition, do they?"

"Directly, no." He stood up and followed her over to the window. "But trust me, Katy. I can sweeten the deal for Green Meadow by making sure we throw a lot of other manufacturing contracts this way."

"Oh, sure." She sighed. "More personalized plastic drinking mugs and plastic hairbrushes. How... creative."

Derek came up behind her and placed his hands on her shoulders. "What's more important to the economic well-being of your town, Katy? Creativity or jobs?"

"That's not a fair question, and you know it."

"Besides—" he turned her slowly around to face him "—we've neglected to mention something even more important than the town of Green Meadow."

"What?"

"*You*, Katy."

"What about me?"

"Why not try being just a little bit selfish?" Derek cupped a hand beneath Katy's chin. Smiling faintly, he lifted her face to meet his gaze. "Have you ever been selfish before? It can be quite healthy sometimes, you know."

She was lost in the silvery depths of Derek's eyes, and started to tremble. "What do you mean?"

"I mean, Katy, you should think about yourself for just a minute." There was a pause. "This deal would make you a very wealthy young woman. One million dollars up front can make life rather pleasant, wouldn't you say?''

"I really haven't given it much thought," she stammered as Derek's other hand left her shoulder and traveled downward to rest on her waist.

"Perhaps it's time you thought about it, then."

There was that captivating luminescence in her green eyes again. "Certain other things are more important than money," Katy asserted.

"Only in books." Derek's fingers were firm and warm against the thin material of her T-shirt. "Only in books, honey. In real life, money is everything."

Katy experienced a slight quiver at his unexpected endearment. "But that sounds so cold-hearted." She tried to keep her voice steady against this oh, so subtle sensual assault. "And I happen to disagree with you. Money is *not* everything."

"Katy, Katy," he declared softly. "You're such a wonderful idealist. That's what comes from living in this quaint, funny village. Street signs that look like candy sticks. Traffic laws out of some comic operetta. Houses that look like huge, pink ice-cream sundaes!"

"You're making fun of me."

Derek shook his head. "No, I'm not. I'm just saying that it's time to wake up from the fairy tale. In the real world, money *is* everything. It's power. It's respect. And it's freedom." There was a strange glitter in his eyes, and then he lowered his mouth onto hers. For a brief, tingling instant, those hard lips brushed against the astonished softness of Katy's. And then, just as quickly, he jerked his mouth away. "Wake up from the fairy tale, Katy," he repeated in a shaky voice. "I say this for your own good."

"And you presume to know what's good for me?" Her mouth was still shocked from his unexpected kiss.

Derek refused to relinquish his grasp on her slender waist. "I have a feeling I'd always know what was good for you, honey."

There was a disturbing undercurrent to his words— a subtle kind of double meaning that caused Katy to tremble almost violently. "And how would you know, Derek?" she said, making a vain attempt to sound indifferent.

"Do you really have to ask that?"

Katy tried to ignore this reply. She cleared her throat. "Maybe I have been a bit hasty. Let me take another look at those papers over there." She gestured blindly toward the kitchen table.

With obvious reluctance, Derek let his arms fall to his sides. "Very well," he agreed, and returned to his chair, trying to ignore the blood pounding in his ears. A moment ago, he'd very nearly lost control and gone over the edge. Katy's lips had been so unbelievably soft and sweet. It had taken every last ounce of willpower not to taste those lips again. That thought was driving him crazy.

Katy had no idea what was going through her companion's troubled mind. All she could think about was being held by Derek, being kissed by him with such taunting briefness. Now the promise of what erotic mastery lay just beneath the cool surface was fully revealed to her, and Katy was forced to confess that she wanted more. She wanted him to kiss her again, only this time, even longer and harder, not just a tantalizing tease of those firm lips. Katy had never experienced such awareness of a man before. She had never wanted J.B. to touch her the way she wanted Derek Randall to touch her.

But back to reality. Katy cleared her throat for the third time. "Explain this contract to me again, won't you?" She made every effort to sound as businesslike as possible.

Derek apparently didn't seem to notice her discomfiture. "Of course," he responded with a curt nod. "I'd be happy to explain anything you want."

"Good."

"No problem." Derek buried his head in the sheaf of papers and tried to remember just why he had come here in the *first* place.

Derek Randall spent the next two hours being true to his word. With commendable patience and clarity he painstakingly explained every aspect of the contract. Katy couldn't help but be impressed by the easy confidence of the man's business demeanor. No wonder he was so obviously successful in his chosen career. Yet there was still something in his personality which reminded Katy of her grandfather. A quality that was difficult to identify. What was it? A kind of stubbornness? A kind of intensity? It certainly wasn't her grandfather's sense of whimsy.

Silently she observed Derek's bent head. Even across the table, she could smell the fresh, herbal scent of the shampoo he must have used that morning. No, Derek Randall was the last person in the world she could describe as being even remotely whimsical.

Just then he looked up from the documents and flashed Katy a smile. "So, how are we doing so far?"

"Oh, fine." There was such incredible warmth in his smile, she thought.

"I'm not going too fast for you, am I?"

"Not at all."

He nodded. "I want to reassure you, Katy. There's no way I intend to allow you to sign any contract you don't fully understand."

"I trust you, Derek."

He gazed at her in surprise. "Do you trust me, Katy? Do you really?"

"Of course," she answered simply. "Why wouldn't I?"

"Yes." Derek's tone was one of wonderment. "I believe you actually mean that."

He sounded so lighthearted, so cheerful that Katy wanted to reach across the table and touch his hand.

But she stifled the impulse, and thought instead about the more puzzling side of Derek Randall. Where did he get that bewildering vulnerability? What had happened in his life to cause the occasional darkness Katy had glimpsed behind the brightness of those wonderful silvery eyes? For example, why did he have such an inexplicable prejudice against toys? It was something that greatly disturbed Katy, because in her mind there was nothing more delightful, more uplifting than a toy. And suddenly, before she could stop herself, she blurted out the question. "Do you mean to tell me you've *never* cared for toys?"

He seemed momentarily taken aback. "What?" Where on earth had the question come from? "Excuse me?"

"Derek Randall, I absolutely refuse to sit here and believe that you have never had a single toy that you loved and simply couldn't live without."

"And what makes you say that?"

"Simple." She crossed her arms in front of her assertively. "There isn't a single living adult who does not have a warm place somewhere in his heart, no matter how deep and forgotten, for that favorite stuffed animal or miniature delivery truck that was waiting under the tree one Christmas."

Derek's smile faded. "And what if that special toy wasn't waiting under the tree at Christmastime? What if there weren't any toys at all?"

Suddenly Katy understood. "That must have been very hard for you, Derek," she said gently.

"Yes," he confessed with an amazing openness that surprised even himself. "It was very hard." It had been years since he'd thought about that particular Christmas morning. Not that it had been any worse than all the other Christmas mornings of his childhood. But it had been the most painful one. It was the Christmas he finally stopped dreaming for the things he could never have.

Katy didn't have to be a mind reader to know what must have occurred. Even now, her heart hurt at the thought of a sad and disappointed little boy with downcast silver eyes. "What was the toy you wanted that Christmas, Derek?"

He shrugged. "Does it matter now? I didn't get it."

"I realize that, but I'd still like to know."

Derek hesitated. "I doubt you ever heard of it." Of course, there was no way Katy could possibly have heard of the obscure little toy he'd longed for so very desperately the year he was nine years old. He glanced across the table at her fresh, young face. Why, she hadn't even been born yet.

"Tell me anyway," she insisted softly.

He sighed. What was it about Katy Kruger that made him want to open his soul and bare the painful secrets hidden in his heart? He'd been an unwanted child, living in a dingy Philadelphia apartment with a father who only came home when he was drunk and a

mother who preferred to ignore him altogether. But at
nine he'd still believed that all parents loved their
children, no matter how the parents' behavior alter-
nated between the aloof and the brutal. That year,
he'd fallen in love with a toy in the window of the local department store. It was a little boy's fantasy. A
magnificent three-story metal parking garage with a
battery-powered elevator to lift all the tiny cars, and a
set of gas pumps outside the entrance to the wonderful structure. *The Casey Parking Garage and Gas
Station,* the writing on the vividly colored cardboard
wrapper read. *So easy to assemble!* And how he'd
dreamed of putting it together all by himself. At nearly
nine, he had envisioned himself as an engineer. The
only problem was that he didn't have the money to buy
it on his own. But his birthday was coming, and for
one miraculous moment, it seemed that *this* was the
year his parents would remember it. His birthday came
and went with scarcely a passing notice. Yet his young,
resilient heart took the disappointment in stride, and
he pinned his hopes instead on Christmas. On Christmas morning, those hopes faded forever. That was
what finally hardened his child's heart to birthdays,
Christmases and all the foolish dreams that don't ever
come true. "You never heard of it, Katy. Just some
obscure little tower of junk that came out for a single
season and disappeared."

"What was the name of the toy, Derek?" she repeated.

He sighed. "The Casey Parking Garage." Funny, he hadn't said the name aloud in over twenty-five years. It sounded so strange to hear it in his deep, grown-up voice instead of a high-pitched child's tone.

"The Casey Parking Garage?" Katy echoed. It sounded so familiar. Where had she heard that name before? "I believe I've heard of it, Derek," she remarked.

"I'm sure," Derek replied, convinced she was only being polite.

Katy didn't press him further. In the back of her mind, she was trying to recall why the toy's name seemed to ring a bell. Well, she would try to remember more about that later. Right now, all she could think of was how grateful she was to Derek for opening up like this for her. She knew he was a person who rarely opened up to anyone. "I'm glad you told me." She smiled. "It means a lot to me."

"Why?"

Before Katy could reply, the telephone rang. As she rose to pick up the receiver on the other side of the room, Derek stopped her with a firm hand on her arm.

"Why does it mean a lot to you, Katy?" His voice seemed strange.

"Because I—" she paused in embarrassment "—I have to answer the phone."

"To hell with the phone!"

"But it's ringing!"

He drew her toward him. "Let it ring!" There was an alien glitter in his eyes. "I want you to tell me why it matters so much to you."

She was pressed against the lean, hard length of him for the second time in as many hours, but now the effect was even more dizzying than before. "Because I—"

"Because you *what*, Katy?"

Her eyes locked with his. "It makes me understand what's *inside* you."

An involuntary shudder went through him. "Why do you care about that?"

Because I care about everything that concerns you! Katy wanted to cry out, but didn't dare. Instead she said, "I hate to think of anyone being unhappy or hurt when he was a child." Her voice was filled with compassion. "I'm sorry you were hurt, Derek. I'm sorry about all those Christmases . . . and probably all those birthdays, too."

"Forget it—" he uttered the words huskily "—it was a long, long time ago." His firm hands came to rest against the small of her back.

"I'm sorry you never got the toy you wished for," she breathed.

"Oh, Katy," Derek rasped. "You're so sweet, so unbelievably sweet!" With a sigh, he lowered his head and claimed her mouth at last.

Never before had Katy experienced such a total assault on her senses. Derek's other brief kiss had been mere child's play, compared to this prolonged, blatantly sensual caress. Without protest, she surrendered to the shattering intensity of Derek's hard lips. As if she had no will of her own, Katy slowly wrapped her arms around his neck and began to respond, kiss for kiss.

Chapter Seven

Somewhere, unnoticed in the distance, the telephone had stopped ringing. Derek gave a muffled exclamation of surprise as he felt Katy press herself against him and wrap her arms around the tense cord of his neck. He'd been hoping for some kind of response, but hadn't asked for heaven.

"God, Katy!" he groaned. "What are you doing to me?"

But Katy was far too lost in the wonder of his long, drugging kisses to answer with words. Instead, she just sighed and abandoned herself to the erotic mastery of Derek's embrace.

But suddenly, that alone wasn't enough for Derek. Kissing Katy, he discovered, was like an addiction, and he wanted more. Much more. "Open your mouth for me, honey!" he urged hoarsely. And then there seemed to be no more barriers between them, as he tasted the moist sweetness within. His hard, probing tongue savored her mouth as if it were honeyed nectar, and then moved on to maddeningly tease the tender flesh of Katy's earlobe.

"Oh!" She gave an involuntary shiver.

Derek stared down at her flushed cheeks and shining eyes. "Do you want me to stop?" he gasped raggedly.

Katy's own voice trembled. "It's just that you make me feel so—" It was hard to find the words.

"How do I make you feel, Katy?"

"So...out of control!" she murmured.

He smiled tenderly. "That's how it's supposed to feel when it's right...all crazy and out of control!" He let his hands travel farther down her body until they found and clasped her hips, pulling her closer against him in an even more intimate embrace. For the first time, Katy was fully aware of the extent of Derek's arousal.

"Can you feel what you're doing to me?" he whispered urgently.

She had never been this close to a man before, not when he was obviously so excited. It was impossible to conceal her astonishment. Katy flushed a bright crimson.

Derek looked at her questioningly. "Are you shocked, Katy?"

She hesitated. The last thing Katy wanted was for this wonderful man to discover how naive and inexperienced she actually was. She was far too painfully aware of most men's attitudes toward unsophisticated virgins. One wrong word from her, and she might send Derek Randall running for the hills. And that was something Katy had no intention of doing under any circumstances. So she mustered all the strength she held in reserve, and forced herself to lie more expertly than she had ever done in the past. It was a white lie that put to shame all the magnificent fibs the Torbor twins had created when they hadn't done their homework assignments. It was a lie that rivaled Ida Johnson's legendary "I swear that traffic light was yellow!" to J. B. Halloran. Lies did not come easily to Katy's lips, but this one was for high stakes. She could not bear it if Derek turned away from her now. So she forced herself to smile vaguely and say, "Shocked? Why, of course not!"

He looked at her strangely. "For a moment I thought you were."

She shook her head. "I'm just suddenly so..." Katy paused deliberately. "So overheated." She hoped that Derek would buy that.

Apparently he did. He rewarded her with a broad smile and a deep sigh. "So, now what, Katy Kruger?"

"I beg your pardon?"

Derek gave a reluctant sigh. "What are we going to do about this?"

Katy didn't quite understand. "About what?"

"I'd say we've got a problem, wouldn't you?" He seemed truly troubled about something.

"What problem are you talking about?" For a minute, Katy thought her lie had backfired, but then it became clear that Derek was concerned about something entirely unexpected.

Firmly he put her away from him. "What are we going to do about J.B.?"

"J.B.?"

There was a pause. "I'd say what's just happened here changes things, wouldn't you, Katy?"

She was quickly growing exasperated. "Changes *what*?"

Derek gazed at her solemnly. "Well, you certainly can't expect things to go on as before, can you?"

The realization of what he was talking about slowly dawned on Katy. "Oh, you don't understand...."

"Of course I understand," he murmured quietly. "J. B. Halloran or me, Katy. You're going to have to choose."

"It's not like that." Katy wanted to laugh. "I already told you that J.B. and I are just *friends*."

Derek was still. "Do you mean that?"

"It'd be a pretty stupid thing to lie about, now wouldn't it?"

"He's a very good-looking man." Derek continued to argue, not quite ready to believe what he was hearing.

"Yes, J.B. is good-looking, but so are you," she countered.

"Oh, please!" he protested. "You don't have to be kind. I know very well how I look." At that moment, Derek wished more than anything that there were no hideous scar and broken nose to mar his features. He'd feel a lot more confident at this moment if *he*, not J. B. Halloran, looked like a Hollywood movie star.

"No, Derek." Katy was suddenly the one who sounded older and wiser. "You know nothing about the way you look." There was a pause. "Haven't you ever heard of the expression 'beauty is in the eye of the beholder'?"

Derek wished more than anything that he could believe her sweet words. If the two of them were back in Manhattan at this very moment, no power on earth would be able to prevent him from making love to Katy. What, he wondered, would it possibly take to get this lovely creature out of here and back to where he stood on more solid footing? To make her forget all about J. B. Halloran? To make her forget about wasting the summer in this backwoods village and return to the city with him? There he could take hours and hours with Katy.... No interruptions. No distractions. Their own private paradise. The idea of having to return to the city and leave Katy behind was enough to make Derek insane with jealousy. Leave her alone with that lovesick sheriff? No way! He would have to think of a plan of defense, and think of it soon!

Suddenly in the distance came the sound of the doorbell, and then footsteps in the hall. No one stood on ceremony in Green Meadow, Derek thought deprecatingly.

"I wonder who that is?" Katy uttered the words just a bit too breathlessly.

Where was a good attack dog when you needed one? Derek wondered in despair. Didn't anybody believe in privacy around here? He turned around in annoyance to see who it was that had the effrontery to shatter his tête-à-tête with Katy.

He should have known just *who* that person would be. *Talk of the devil!*

"I can only stay a minute." J. B. Halloran stood in the kitchen and drew himself up to his full height of six feet, five inches. The way he leaned casually against the counter, with his gun belt dangling from his hips, J.B. seemed like a man who radiated inner confidence.

"What's up, J.B.?" Katy asked quickly, hoping that her old friend wouldn't notice the flush on her cheeks.

"Oh, I was just in the neighborhood," he practically drawled, "and wondered if you could spare a cup of coffee."

Katy stared at him in astonishment. J. B. Halloran had never stopped by for a cup of coffee in his life!

"Uh, sure," she said, and walked over to the stove, where the percolator stood steaming.

"So, what kind of mileage do you get on that Buick?" J.B. asked Derek suddenly.

"Great. Just fine," Derek said, a constriction in his throat. Whom was this guy trying to kid? J. B. Halloran had seen the beige Regal parked in the Kruger driveway, and had stopped by to investigate.

"Staying in town long, Derek?" he continued conversationally.

"Until I finish my business."

J.B. didn't blink an eye. "And what business is that?"

Derek was fighting every impulse to tell the younger man to go take a running jump in the lake. It wasn't that Derek was a particularly vengeful person, or that in other circumstances he wouldn't find J. B. Halloran a pretty decent guy. But at this moment, he knew very well what was going on. The sheriff of Green Meadow was making it quite clear to the out-of-town visitor that he held a prior claim on Katy Kruger.

"Derek represents the company that wants to buy the rights to the Baby Katy," the object of the tense little standoff interjected. She brought J.B. a mug of coffee.

"Thanks, honey." J.B. smiled his vaguest smile yet, and Katy stiffened.

What had gotten into the man? Since when had he ever gone in for calling her *honey*?

Derek felt jealousy sear his gut. It was obvious that he had lost this round. It was time to retreat, regroup his forces, and figure out a new strategy. J.B. certainly hadn't won the war yet. With Derek's considerable power and influence in the business world, there was more than one way to get him out of the picture. How would this country lawman like a plum security job on a private island in the Bahamas?

"So, what does your company intend to do with the doll?" J.B. stared steadily at Derek.

"Mass-produce it for the new youth market." He stared back unflinchingly.

"Sounds real fascinating." The police officer gazed into his coffee cup. "You like dolls, Derek?"

"I don't know much about them, actually."

J.B. set down his coffee cup. "The Katy is a very special doll. It would be quite a shame if your company were to mishandle it...treat it like just any other doll." He looked up again. "People around here have a lot of sentiment tied up in that little Katy. It would really upset them if the management of your company were to underestimate what a quality product they were dealing with."

"I agree with you, J.B."

"I'm glad you do, Derek." He reached into his pocket and removed his sunglasses. "I hate to drink and run, Katy, but I'd better get back to work."

"Uh, right." She nodded at her old friend, still completely mystified by his impromptu visit. What was going on with him? And why had he been rambling on and on about the Katy doll? J. B. Halloran had never cared a hill of beans for the Baby Katy or any doll, for that matter. He was probably the most unsentimental human being of all her friends and acquaintances.

J.B. slid the lenses onto the bridge of his perfect nose and gave Derek a nod. "Nice chatting with you."

"You, too, J.B." Derek twisted his lips in dry amusement. Yes, the battle lines had most definitely been drawn, he thought. And although Katy had surrendered so sweetly to his kisses, Derek remained more unconvinced than ever that she and this other man were merely friends. *Friends.* That word took in much territory and a broad array of meanings. This J. B. Halloran was nothing if not persistent. And as long as the handsome young law enforcement officer remained in Green Meadow, he would definitely cramp Derek's style. Oh sure, once the summer was over, and Katy was safely back in Manhattan for the fall semester, he thought smugly, it would be a completely different story. But a good deal could happen between now and the end of August, especially if this J. B.

Halloran was the type who wanted to marry and raise a family. He certainly had that "settling down" look in his eyes when he cast a glance in Katy's direction. Derek's jaw tightened. The sooner J. B. Halloran was out of the picture, the better. Didn't Consolidated's overseas division need a new chief of security at its headquarters in Brazil?

In the end, it was Leo Kruger who urged Katy to sign the contract with Consolidated Industries. She was a bit surprised at his sudden capitulation, but decided that it was wise not to probe too deeply. In fact, the old man had reached his decision while fishing that day with Whitey Wilson. Sitting at the water's edge, he had realized that life was short, too short. He'd rest better at night, knowing that Katy would always have a tidy nest egg for her future. His declaration that accepting Consolidated's offer made sound business sense was so convincing that Katy never guessed what a painful decision it had really been for the elderly toy maker. Secretly he felt like Leonardo da Vinci selling his Mona Lisa to a paint-by-numbers concession. It was like parting with a treasured possession. But it would mean that his only grandchild would be well provided for throughout the rest of her life. And that was worth everything. All he could bequeath her now was a run-down factory on the verge of bankruptcy. He hadn't even been able to pay her college tuition, and that had hurt him even more than the pain of selling out.

Late in the afternoon, Derek was delighted when he received a phone call from Katy, informing him that she had decided to accept his offer. Winning always gave him great satisfaction, and while it pleased the executive to chalk up another success, this time he was pleased for another reason, as well. Agreeing to sign over the copyright meant that Katy would have to fly down to Consolidated's New York office for the day. What better way to get Katy alone and far away from her "friend" J. B. Halloran, even if it was only for a single night?

"Naturally," he'd informed her, "the company will put you up at its own expense in one of the better hotels in the city."

"Oh, you mean I'd be staying there overnight?" Katy had sounded surprised.

"Of course," Derek had replied. "It would be a terribly long day for you, otherwise." He paused for a moment. "Is there a problem with that, Katy?"

"Not at all," she'd said. But for some reason, the idea of spending even one night away from Green Meadow in the company of Derek Randall was rather unnerving.

It was arranged that the two of them leave for the city on the following morning. This plan seemed to make the most sense all around. Derek appeared anxious to resolve the deal as soon as possible, and besides, in less than two weeks' time, Katy's attentions would be completely engaged by her staff duties at Camp Silverwood.

So that night, Katy tried to go to bed early and get some rest for the busy day ahead. However, she found this to be impossible. Katy paced restlessly in her bedroom. Finally she went over to the window, pulled back the filmy lace curtains and stared up at the waning moon. She couldn't help replaying the events of that incredible morning over and over again in her mind.

He had kissed her with such passion and persuasive skill that it had left no doubt in Katy's mind as to Derek's intentions. For all of her naiveté and lack of experience, Katy would have had to be a fool not to get the man's subtle erotic message. Given the time and the opportunity, Derek obviously intended to carry that kiss even further.

The prospect of making love with him made Katy shudder deliciously. Everything was happening so fast. She had grown up with the ingrained belief that a woman should wait until she was in love before giving herself fully to a man. Well, she had waited. She had waited for more than twenty-four years, and it had seemed like forever. And then Derek had come along. Things had happened with such insane speed that Katy could scarcely believe it. She had only known the man for one week, less than that, if you considered how much of that week they had spent together. But what was she feeling inside for Derek Randall, if it wasn't love? No other man had ever been able to wreak such havoc on her emotions before. No other man had been able to turn her knees to jelly, just by looking in her direction. But most important, no other man had ever before evoked such a physical response from her, merely with a kiss. Love was not a word that Katy had ever used with the carelessness of her friends, but she knew now that she must have been in love with Derek almost from the moment she'd met him. From the moment at the party, when he had so effortlessly slung Marvin Feeney's unconscious body across his shoulder and insisted upon driving her home, Katy had known that falling in love with Derek was only a step away.

But what did Derek feel for her, other than desire? Katy had no way of knowing for sure. He hadn't referred again to the brief interlude, nor did he make another attempt to kiss her before leaving, later that morning. It occurred to Katy that Derek might have regretted that he'd kissed her in the first place. Then J.B. had had to show up like that and shatter the moment. Well, Katy didn't pretend to understand either man. All she understood was the dictates of her own heart.

To love a man as sophisticated as Derek Randall would probably lead to heartbreak, but Katy felt like a moth drawn to a flame. Love was more than sex or possession. She cared about what was inside the man, as well. She would be happy to know Derek, even just as a friend. She loved not only the man, but the little boy who had been so terribly disillusioned all those Christmases ago. Even if he had never taken her into his arms and kissed her that morning, Katy still would have wanted to heal the bitter memory of a childhood so devoid of joy. Of a cherished, longed-for toy that had never been received. The Casey Parking Garage had been Derek Randall's magical touchstone, and it had eluded him. How Katy wished she had it in her power to turn the clock back and set things right! If only it were possible to travel back through time and put the Casey Parking Garage underneath little Derek Randall's Christmas tree more than a quarter century ago! Katy shook her head regretfully and climbed back into bed. Something, however, lingered in the recesses of her mind.

Several hours later, Katy awakened suddenly and sat bolt upright in the canopied bed. Casey's Parking Garage! No wonder she'd thought the name had sounded familiar when Derek had mentioned it to her this morning! She threw back the coverlet and rose from the bed. Pulling on a robe and slippers, Katy crept quietly into the hallway and made her way upstairs into the attic. She clicked on the light and glanced about the cavernous room, which ran the entire length of the house. The attic looked like a warehouse, jammed from floor to rafters with stacks of toys and games, still wrapped in their original boxes. These boxes were of all shapes and sizes, slightly yellowed with age and coated with a thin layer of dust.

It took some long moments of rummaging through these piles, not to mention the cobwebs, before Katy gave a triumphant cry. She had found what she was looking for. Buried beneath some other cartons was a box labeled Special Order. In tiny lettering in the corner of the aging storage box was printed Casey's Parking Garage and Filling Station—One Doz. Ct.

Before the incredible popularity of the Katy doll and the development of its plastics line, the Kruger factory produced items of tin or cold-pressed steel. In those early years, her grandfather had created such a vast assortment of toys, some exclusively manufactured for department store chains under their own labels, that it had been difficult to keep track of them all. The Casey garage set was just one of many such special orders.

Katy carefully slid out the box from the neat pile, opened the flaps, and removed one of the individual packages. It was still covered in the original cellophane, somewhat yellowed, but otherwise none the worse for wear. She gave an odd smile. Who would have thought that a simple little toy that had lain unappreciated in an attic for all these years could mean so much to someone else? Who knows? she thought. Maybe it was possible in this case to turn back the clock and make things right for Derek Randall. Smiling her own secret smile, Katy placed the package carefully under her arm and went back downstairs to bed.

Chapter Eight

Derek showed up early the next morning to drive Katy to the airport, and he seemed more relaxed than she had ever seen him. Dressed with his usual easy elegance in the perfectly cut gray suit and silk tie, Derek appeared somewhat out of place on the steps of the pink and white Victorian house. Although he made no attempt to kiss Katy hello or even to touch her hand, his smile at seeing her was a genuine one. His eyes skimmed approvingly over her outfit. Katy was wearing her best dress, a simple knit in a flattering hue of jade. With a short, matching jacket and leather belt, it was the same classic outfit she had worn for all special occasions since high school graduation. Needless to say, special occasions hadn't come along very often, and the jade outfit still looked good, even after six years.

"You look very pretty," he murmured.

"Thank you," Katy responded quietly, stifling the impulse to add that *he* looked just as devastatingly attractive as ever, and by the way, she also happened to be in love with him. This blazing new inner knowledge dazzled, yet frightened Katy. It made her vulnerable in a disturbing new way, a way she was for the moment reluctant to confront.

"So, are you ready to go?" Derek inquired.

"Uh, of course." Katy prayed he couldn't read the alarming new jumble of feelings inside her.

"What is it, Katy?" He quirked an eyebrow and stared at her, puzzled.

"So, how long will this whole thing take?" Leo Kruger interjected curiously. "Did you say one night?"

"Perhaps two," Derek answered casually. "It all depends."

"On what?"

"Several things." He rested his gaze on Katy. Quickly, though, Derek seemed to remember where he was. "If all goes smoothly, Katy could be back tomorrow. But there's always red tape. You know lawyers."

"Well, sure." Leo Kruger nodded in agreement. "Those big-city lawyers always know how to stick a fly in the molasses, don't they?" He bent over and kissed

Katy on the cheek. "But don't let them get the better of you, dear. Remember, you're a *Kruger*!"

"Right, Gramps." Katy nodded obediently.

The old man glanced over at Derek. "Look after my granddaughter, Mr. Randall."

"Of course." Derek gave a vague smile.

"Manhattan is a dangerous place, but try and tell Katy that. She never listens to a word I say."

"That's not true, Gramps!" Katy protested weakly.

"All I know is, you *love* Manhattan!"

"I also happen to love Green Meadow, as you well know."

The elderly toy maker shrugged his shoulders. "I only know that you'd rather *live* in Manhattan."

Derek gazed at her in mild surprise. "Is that so? How very interesting." He smiled a secret inner smile.

"Yes, it's a wild place, that New York City, Mr. Randall. Take good care of her for me."

Derek's silvery glance rested on Katy's slender body. "Oh, I'll take good care of her, Mr. Kruger. You can depend on it."

Leo Kruger's eyes narrowed speculatively. "I sincerely hope so."

There was a subtle interplay between the two men the meaning of which Katy completely missed. She had chosen that precise moment to reach down for her suitcase.

"Oh, let me carry that." Derek leaned over and took the luggage from her grasp. "This is heavy," he remarked with amusement. "What do you have in here, bricks?"

There was something very special in the weekender, in fact, but Katy merely smiled evasively and answered, "Oh, just the usual things...toothbrush, comb, forty-pound weights."

Derek grinned and glanced down at his expensive gold watch. "Well, we'd better get going, if we want to catch that flight."

They said their final goodbyes to Leo Kruger and walked down the steps to the beige Buick. Derek stowed the suitcase in the trunk, the two of them got into the car and drove away. As the car disappeared into the distance, the old man stared at the horizon with a strange expression on his face.

Derek turned to Katy a moment later and inquired casually, "How does your friend feel about this little trip to New York?"

"What friend?"

Derek sighed impatiently. "You know very well *what* friend. Why play games?"

Katy paused thoughtfully. "Oh, you mean J.B.?"

"Of course I mean J.B." He gave a deprecating twist of the lips. "I'm surprised Mr. Wyatt Earp doesn't come racing after me now, sirens and all, and bodily prevent you from leaving town. That is, after he has *me* tossed in jail for traveling one mile over the unposted speed limit!"

Was he actually jealous? Katy wondered with a leap of her heart. Then she replayed the annoyance in his voice when he accused her of playing games. Katy simply didn't know how to play games. It just wouldn't occur to her. She was in love with this man, but it didn't mean that Katy didn't find his behaviour absolutely exasperating at times. "I don't play games, Derek Randall," she announced with uncharacteristic coldness.

He raised an eyebrow. "No, Katy?"

"As a matter of fact, I resent such an accusation."

He briefly took his eyes from the country road and noted her solemn expression. "Why deny it, honey?" He shrugged carelessly. "All women play games. They have since the beginning of time. It goes with the territory."

"Not *my* territory." Katy crossed her arms in growing irritation. "And another thing I don't do, either, is lie."

The unexpected harshness of her reaction seemed to startle him. "Is it possible that I've offended you, Katy?"

She tossed back her hair defiantly. "Quite possible." There was a pause. "Rather a strong *probability*, in fact." There was an even longer pause. "Why not just call it a certainty, and have done with it, Mr. Randall?"

"*Mr.* Randall?" he exclaimed. "Then I really must have put my foot in my mouth!" Noting her continued silence, Derek gave her a conciliatory smile. "If I've been insensitive, Katy, forgive me. It's just that I find this entire situation somewhat bewildering."

Katy turned to look at him. "What situation?"

He shook his head. "Do I have to spell it out? I enjoyed kissing you yesterday morning, Katy. I like to think you enjoyed kissing me back, too."

Just to hear him refer to those exquisite moments in the kitchen made Katy tingle. "I did enjoy it, Derek," she confessed in a low voice.

A light flickered briefly across Derek's hard features. "I thought you did, Katy. That's why I'm bewildered. I wish you'd explain your relationship with J. B. Halloran."

Oh, not *that* again! How many times would she have to explain this to Derek, before something finally sank into that thick cranium of his? Her cheeks flushed a faint but indignant tint of pink. "You know what, Derek? I'm getting pretty darn tired of 'explaining' my so-called relationship with J.B. Would you like to know the truth?"

His grip on the steering wheel tightened. "That's all I ever wanted. Go ahead, Katy. I'm all ears."

She stared out at the passing scenery. It was all so green and tranquil. Such a vivid contrast to the turmoil churning inside her. "Ever since I can remember, J.B. was the town hero. In junior high, every girl had a mad crush on him."

"Including you," Derek interjected cynically.

"Including me," she confessed with embarrassment. "You asked me to tell you the truth, didn't you?"

"Yes, I did," came the curt reply. "I assume there's more."

Katy sighed. "J.B. always treated me like a little sister. Three years ago, when he came back from the marines, I'd just graduated from college. Suddenly he considered me a grown-up. A friend he could talk to about things. But he never even asked me out on a date until a week ago. And that's the truth."

"So what you're telling me—" Derek's voice was tinged with sarcasm "—is that you're friends who happen to date each other. It appears that we're back at square one, Katy."

She shook her head in utter exasperation. "Oh, I just give up, Derek Randall. I absolutely give up trying to explain anything at all to you! You deliberately misunderstand everything I say!"

"Oh, really?" he retorted. "As it happens, I understand everything you say quite well. All *too* well, in fact."

They continued the drive to the airport in virtual silence, exchanging only the vaguest of conversational pleasantries. By the time the two of them boarded the La Guardia-bound commuter flight, though, some of the frostiness between them had mercifully thawed. The truth was, Derek found himself unable to remain annoyed with Katy for any length of time. All he had to do was glance at her lovely face and sweetly indignant expression, and continuing to treat her brusquely made him feel like Ebenezer Scrooge.

Katy, on the other hand, just had to be on the receiving end of a genuine Derek Randall conciliatory smile, and felt it was positively shrewish to remain cool toward the man. After all, his behavior might sometimes be frustrating and confusing, but her knees still turned to jelly when he looked at her with any degree of warmth. How could she feign indifference to the man she just happened to be head over heels in love with?

Oh, sure, Katy reasoned ironically as they sat in the departure lounge, waiting for their flight to be called. Sure, it would be so easy to clear up any misunderstanding simply by saying, "Are you nuts, Derek? I happen to date J. B. Halloran because he *asked* me. The truth is, *you*'re the one I'm in love with. How do you like *those* apples?" Oh, right. She was really going to bare her soul like that to Derek Randall! She'd never told a man she was in love with him before, and she wasn't about to make a fool of herself now. Particularly not when she hadn't an inkling of the man's feelings toward *her*.

Katy pursed her lips and tried to ignore the scent of Derek's after-shave wafting toward her in the moist heat of the terminal. It was a heady, masculine aroma.

So undeniably a part of *this* man. She shifted uncomfortably in her seat.

"They're calling our flight," Derek repeated for the third time, his deep voice finally piercing the haze of Katy's thoughts.

"Yes, of course," she murmured quickly, and stood up to follow her tall, gaunt companion toward the boarding gate. Being in love certainly wasn't what it was cracked up to be, she told herself with disdain. Katy didn't like the vulnerable way it made her feel. No, she didn't like that part at all.

But once they were seated on the plane, and the craft began to taxi slowly toward the runway, Katy's mind was occupied by something else completely. Something that effectively washed away, if just for a moment, all other emotions. It started just as soon as the seat belts were securely fastened and the reality of what was about to happen finally struck Katy. She was on an airplane! An airplane that would shortly take off! Katy turned as pale as a sheet.

"What's the matter?" Derek looked at her curiously.

"Nothing!" she said, a bit too loudly.

"Are you still upset with me for those things I said in the car? I apologize, Katy. I suppose I don't have the right to tell you what to do. Or whom to see." There was a pause. "I don't have that right," he repeated softly. "Do I, Katy?"

"Flight attendants, prepare for takeoff." The pilot's voice filtered over the public address system. And Katy's fingers dug involuntarily into the armrests.

Realization dawned on Derek at that moment. His silver eyes narrowed. "Are you afraid of flying?"

"You could say that." She gave a nervous jerk of her head.

Just then, the airplane began its rapid acceleration toward the end of the runway, and the entire cabin pitched upward. Blindly Katy reached out and grabbed Derek's shoulder, her fingers digging into the soft wool of his gray suit.

"It's okay," he assured her with a faint smile, "there's nothing to worry about. We're safely airborne now."

"How do you know?" Her eyes remained tightly shut.

"Take a look out your window." The amusement was evident in his voice. "Those are clouds out there."

"I'll take your word for it."

Derek gave her a strange look. "How often do you fly, Katy?"

She stared down at the floor. "Never."

There was a pause. "Are you saying that this is the first time you've ever been on an airplane?"

"Yes." The answer was dragged from her lips.

He shook his head in amazement. "There's no end to your surprises, is there?" His hand gently removed the fingers still gripping the material of his jacket, and clasped them reassuringly. "Listen. Flying happens to be a lot safer than driving, believe me."

Katy drew a deep breath. "I don't mean to be such a wimp," she declared. "It's just that being this high up is a new sensation. It takes some getting used to, you know."

Derek continued to hold her hand through most of the flight. He was so patient and understanding that it seemed so difficult to believe that this was the same man who had been so intimidating just an hour before. During the landing, when the wheels and wing flaps made those terrifyingly unfamiliar noises, Derek became even more reassuring.

"Here," he drew her against his shoulder soothingly. "Just relax like this, honey. Everything is going to be all right." As he felt Katy's tense body begin to go limp against his, he felt a surge of triumph. How could he ask for anything better than this? Derek thought. Here Katy was, pressed up alongside him so trustingly. This was a completely new sensation for Derek Randall. No woman had ever brought out his protective instincts before. It was not only a refreshingly new experience, but a distinctly pleasurable one, as well.

The meeting at Consolidated Industries' Manhattan office was scheduled for noon. Besides Katy and Derek, the corporate attorney was present, along with a balding, red-faced man named Lester Winters, whom Derek introduced as the vice president in charge of marketing. This was an impressive title, to be sure, but Katy decided that she didn't care for the man. The more enthusiastically he sang the praises of the marketing potential of a reissued Baby Katy, the more obnoxious he became. And as if that alone wasn't enough, she also did not care for the way Mr. Lester Winters, who wore a wide gold wedding ring displayed prominently on his chubby finger, flirted almost beyond the limits of good taste. There was the kind of discomfort Katy experienced when Derek Randall stared so intimately at her, but that was a delicious kind. She had never found Derek's attentions unpleasant. But Les Winters stared at her with what might almost be referred to as a leer, and Katy just wished the lecherous executive would dissolve into the woodwork.

When all the aspects of the contract had been thoroughly reviewed, and Katy was ready to sign the papers, Les Winters leaned across the table and said, "A million-dollar contract is certainly something to celebrate, little lady. How about you and me going out later for a drink?"

Katy stiffened, but before she could reply, Derek shot his colleague a glance of silver ice so sharp that it shattered any present or future fantasies Les Winters might have been entertaining about the attractive redhead sitting in the opposite chair.

"Miss Kruger already has plans," Derek informed the marketing VP with a coldness that practically bordered on contempt.

Any other time, Katy might have resented a man presuming to answer for her, but right now she was frankly relieved that Derek had come to her rescue. In addition, Katy was forced to admit that it was not an altogether unpleasant sensation to hear Derek sound almost...possessive. Was that just an overactive imagination? Very likely, it was wishful thinking on Katy's part. On the other hand, there was no mistaking the note of barely suppressed anger in Derek's voice, when he put Lester Winters in his place.

After the contracts had all been signed and duly notarized, Katy's doubts were permanently set to rest an hour later, when Derek insisted on walking her the short distance to her hotel.

"Thanks for seeing me through that meeting," she said as they stood in the bustling lobby.

"I honestly believe you won't regret signing that deal," he said simply. "It was the wisest course to follow, Katy...sentiment aside."

"That remains to be seen," she answered vaguely, "but actually, I wasn't referring to the contract."

"What, then?"

Katy gazed at him with a bright expression in her green eyes. "Thanks for helping me deflect that overbearing colleague of yours."

Derek's mouth tightened. "Les Winters has got a lot of nerve! He's married, with four children!"

"Well, in any case, I appreciate your stepping in like that and telling him I already had plans."

He shrugged. "But you do have plans, Katy."

"Oh, is that a fact?"

"Absolutely." He smiled down at her confidently. "Aren't we having dinner tonight?"

"I don't know. *Are* we?"

"I've got to get back to the office, but if it's convenient for you, how about if I come by at around seven-thirty? I'd like to take you out to a favorite restaurant of mine."

"All right—" she nodded in assent "—but I hope you realize this is the only dress I brought with me." Katy gestured hesitantly at her jade outfit.

Derek's silver glance rested on the clinging curves of the attractive knit. "It'll do just fine. Believe me." Idly he brushed a loose strand of red hair away from her cheek. It was almost as if he had to force himself to say goodbye then, and leave her standing alone in the plush lobby.

During the meeting, the staff at Consolidated had sent out for sandwiches and coffee, so Katy was able to survive quite comfortably until dinner without any hunger pangs. Quickly she changed into her jeans and sneakers and left the hotel. It was a clear, warm afternoon in June. An altogether glorious time of year to be in New York City. More than anything, Katy wanted to take her favorite walk up Fifth Avenue and past Central Park to the Metropolitan Museum of Art. Although she had only been away for little more than a week, it had been quite a while since Katy had taken the time to retrace the steps of her favorite stroll. Past those tree-fringed blocks bordering the park with the book vendors, the young mothers sitting on the benches with their toddlers, and the teenagers holding those giant, blaring radios poised so effortlessly against their ears. Katy reached the massive front entrance of the museum and paused to throw a penny into the glistening fountain.

Since first coming to this place, Katy had always made the same wish. In the past, this wish had been of a somewhat nonspecific nature. But now, Katy was able to focus more clearly on its object. Her thoughts lingered on a tanned, angular face with piercing silver-gray eyes and a jagged white scar. The penny hit the water with an almost imperceptible splash. For a moment, Katy gazed pensively at the shining copper coin as it glinted in the sunlight. Sometimes, she reminded herself hopefully, wishes did come true.

Derek knocked on her door at precisely seven-thirty. The man was nothing if not incredibly prompt, Katy thought with a smile. Somehow this fitted the superbly efficient and authoritative businessman she had seen at work during today's meeting at Consolidated Industries. It had been so easy to see that in his own high-powered environment, the self-assured young executive shone like a star. It was evident that Derek Randall commanded the respect of everyone around him. He might have seemed somewhat like a fish out of water in a tiny, out-of-the-way village such as Green Meadow, but here, within the glass and steel super-structure of Consolidated, Derek Randall was most definitely in his element.

Katy opened the door, to see that Derek had changed into a navy pinstripe suit and crisp white oxford shirt. For just a moment he stood there looking down at her. "Hello, Katy," he murmured, taking in every detail of her appearance as if he had never seen her before.

"Hello, Derek." She gave a bright nod, unable to understand why the butterflies were churning in her stomach once again. How could he seem to stare into her soul like that? Why did the man make her feel as if she were wearing something far more exotic than the old jade knit dress and the lightest touch of lipstick and mascara?

"I hope you're hungry," he remarked with an almost forced casualness.

"In fact, I am."

Then he smiled, and the smile seemed to light up his entire face. And suddenly it seemed like the most natural and spontaneous gesture when he just leaned over and gave Katy a brief hug, followed by an even briefer brush of his hard lips against Katy's mouth. "Ready?"

"Ready." She pulled away quickly, unwilling to let him see the hot flush in her cheeks. "I'll just get my jacket."

The restaurant where Derek had made reservations was a dimly lit establishment that occupied the two lower floors of an Upper Eastside brownstone. It was called Mario's, and the proprietor was obviously well acquainted with Derek Randall. He was a soulful-eyed Sicilian, who greeted the young executive like a long-lost relative and bestowed upon Katy a long stream of effusive compliments, all of which, however, seemed quite sincere.

The restaurateur escorted them to a prime table, set with fine crystal and crisp white linen. With a wink, he pulled out one of the leather-backed chairs for Katy and, once she was comfortably seated, he leaned over and whispered something into Derek's ear, before disappearing into the kitchen.

"What was that all about?" she inquired curiously.

Derek smiled. "Mario is rather smitten with you, Katy. He called you *bellissima*." There was a pause, then he added, "Not that it's necessary to translate, but I happen to agree with him wholeheartedly. You are very beautiful."

Katy's heart began hammering again. "Thank you." Derek's compliments had a way of going to her head.

He quirked an eyebrow. "I still make you nervous, don't I?"

Before she could answer, Mario returned with a bottle of Chablis, uncorked it with deft skill, and paused confidently while Derek sampled it with an approving nod. "Excellent, is it not, Mr. Randall?"

"As always," Derek answered and waited for the proprietor to pour some of the golden liquid into Katy's crystal goblet. As Mario walked away with a satisfied smile, Derek observed, "Does he remind you of Roscoe, by any chance?"

Katy gave a faint smile. "Not in the least." She lifted her glass. "What shall we toast, Derek?"

He paused significantly. "That's an interesting question. But for the moment, why not just toast the signing of a million-dollar contract? Today you are a woman of independent means, Katherine Kruger." He raised his own goblet and carefully tapped it against hers. "Here's to the beginning of all wonderful things for you, Katy."

There was something very touching in his words, and Katy was thoughtful as she accepted the toast. "I wonder how much one million dollars can change a person's life."

He studied her silently. "It's something to consider." To himself, he wondered if the money truly would change Katy in a radical way. On one hand, he would be delighted to see her cut herself loose from all the ties that bound her to that quaint but remote upstate village. Then again, it would be a shame if Katy Kruger were to become like so many other wealthy young women of his acquaintance. Spoiled. Self-indulgent. Blasé. Was there really a risk that anything could take away the sweetness and lack of guile that seemed the essence of Katy's appeal?

"I don't intend to spend all that money just on myself." Katy let the golden liquid warm her throat. She seldom drank wine, and it was a heady feeling. Each sip seemed to send a warm glow more and more brightly throughout her entire body. Down to her toes, in fact. "But it will mean I can quit pulling double shifts of waiting tables during the semester and really concentrate on classes."

"It hasn't been easy for you, has it?" he murmured, touching his fingers tentatively to hers across the table.

"I've been more fortunate than most," she reflected honestly, enjoying the sensation of his firm fingers on her skin. "Not that I won't be extremely pleased to see the last of that cockroach-infested shoe box I now call an apartment."

Derek's hand tightened on hers. "So you'll be moving back to the city as planned?"

"Most definitely." Katy was unaware that her wine glass had been mysteriously refilled. She took another sip. "Why would you even doubt it, Derek?"

"Oh, I have my reasons," he answered enigmatically.

She shrugged. "The truth is, I love the pace of life here. Green Meadow is a delightful place to come home to, but if you're going to be an artist, there's nothing like the vibrant and exiting mix of cultures one finds here. For all its flaws, I'll take Manhattan, just like the words of the song."

"I'm glad to hear you say that." His voice was deep.

Katy looked at him questioningly. "Why?"

"Because, Katy Kruger, I would miss you very much if you weren't here."

This seemed such an astonishing confession that she could only stare back. "You would?"

"Most definitely." He hesitated for a moment, then drew a breath. "In fact, I—"

But at that precise instant Mario reappeared on the scene, and whatever Derek had been about to say was destined to remain a mystery. At least for the present. After taking their orders for antipasto and the house specialty, the *linguine di frutti di mare*, he gestured in the direction of a small dance floor. "Later on, of course, is the music." The wiry, attractive proprietor cocked his head questioningly at Derek. "This time, Mr. Randall, you will dance?"

"Of course," Derek said quietly, watching Katy's face, "if you'd be willing, Katy." There was a pause. "Mario's cousins have a trio," he explained. "They're rather good, actually."

The thought of being held in Derek's arms was always an appealing one, as far as she was concerned. To be able to dance with this wonderful man was more than Katy could have asked for. "That sounds very nice."

Mario gave Katy a conspiratorial wink. "*Signorina,* that is excellent! Never before will Mr. Randall agree to dance with anyone he brings to my *ristorante,* but then, never before has he brought anyone so lovely!" He paused appreciatively. "Such hair and eyes! *Bellissima!*"

After he walked away, there was an embarrassed silence.

"You don't have to dance, if you'd rather not," Katy said finally.

Derek shook his head. "You don't understand." There was an odd expression in his silvery eyes. "I've never wanted to dance with anyone else here before."

"You wouldn't mind?" Even as Katy asked the question, she felt a sharp stab of pain at the idea of him bringing other women to this special place, the place he called his favorite restaurant. She wondered how many of them there had been. Again she conjured up the disturbing image of Lorna, and just as quickly discarded the picture from her mind.

"How could I ever mind dancing with you, Katy?"
he inquired hoarsely.

There was something so tantalizing about his tone
that she felt the warmth flooding through her, a
warmth that owed nothing to the wine.

It was a delightful dinner, probably the most pleasurable one ever in Katy's recollection. The seafood
linguine was superb, with its delicate blend of clams,
mussels, sliced scallops and shrimp. It was, however,
laced quite generously with fresh crushed garlic. When
Katy casually mentioned this to Derek, he gave an almost playful shrug.

"I thought you understood that garlic is never a
problem when *two* people both have eaten it," he
teased.

"Is that so, Derek Randall?" she shot back.

He grinned. "As a matter of fact, I intend to enjoy
the garlic quite thoroughly." He continued to eat his
entrée with enthusiasm, smiling an even broader smile
when Katy gave a sigh and followed suit.

During the rest of the meal, Derek ordered yet another bottle of Chablis and continued to ask Katy
more questions about her life in Manhattan and the art
career she hoped to pursue.

"My dream is to one day write and illustrate children's books," she confessed.

Derek shook his head. "For some reason, I am no
at all surprised, Katy. Not at all. It's so very like you

to involve yourself in a career that embraces youth and whimsy.''

Whimsy, thought Katy. There was that word again. When Derek used it, he clearly implied that this was a quality quite alien to him. Once more, this thought saddened Katy. She wondered if Derek Randall's dreary outlook could ever be transformed.

How serious she looked all of a sudden, Derek mused to himself. He carelessly downed another glass of wine. He had been to Mario's hundreds of times over the years it seemed, often in the company of an attractive female, but watching Katy across the table now in the dim candlelight, it struck Derek that he had never until now felt wildly romantic. Sitting here with Katy was giving him the craziest ideas. He silently observed the play of the candlelight on her red hair and bright eyes. Right then Derek was seized with the most dizzying urge to ask Katy to run away for a week in Acapulco. And then he was seized with an even wilder impulse. He wanted to lean across the table right at this moment and persuade Katherine Kruger to move in with him. Make her forget all about going back to that insignificant camp counselor job in Green Meadow this summer. Make her forget all about finding a brand-new apartment in the city this fall. Unless that brand-new apartment happened to be *his*. It occurred to Derek that living with Katy might be exceedingly delightful.

Just then, the three-piece band, which had quietly set up in the corner of the room, began to warm up. In the trio were a pianist, a drummer and a bass player. Soon the restaurant was filled with the strains of a familiar pop ballad. Couples began to drift onto the tiny dance floor. Derek extended his hand to Katy and smiled. "Would you care to dance?" he murmured.

"Yes, I would." She slowly drew herself up from the chair and allowed Derek to guide her toward the dance floor. Perhaps it was the music, or perhaps it was the wine, but as he pulled her into the circle of his arms, Katy felt as if she were floating away on a gossamer cloud.

Chapter Nine

The music continued to play. To the strains of an old Cole Porter standard, Derek led Katy around the small dance floor with an unexpected grace of movement.

"You're a very good dancer," she murmured against the soft wool of his jacket.

"Thank you," came the deep reply. "The feeling is mutual." Until now, Derek had held Katy at a discreet distance, one hand clasped around her slender waist, the other one holding her hand in midair in precisely the correct ballroom pose. But in Derek's opinion that had gone on long enough. When else would he have a better excuse to hold Katy even closer? Without another word, Derek brought the other hand down to rest on Katy's waist, and drew her even more closely into the circle of his embrace. Once again, Katy felt herself pressed tightly against the lean hardness of Derek's body. The clean, male smell of him made her senses tingle. At first, Katy had perched her hands somewhat tentatively on Derek's shoulders, but as the drugging rhythm of the music made her even more relaxed and confident, she slowly allowed her fingers to reach up toward his neck.

"Katy." Derek gave a sigh of pleasure and buried his face in the softness of her hair. It smelled faintly of a familiar flower scent that seemed fresh and light. Distinctly *Katy*, he decided.

"What?" she whispered into the fine cotton of his oxford shirt. He felt warm and vital through the thin material. She could almost hear his heart beating.

"Everything about you is so soft and sweet!" he breathed against the silkiness of her hair. And then they were no longer dancing, but moving slowly to the hypnotic beat of the music.

There was an innocent eroticism in the way they swayed back and forth on the crowded dance floor. "It's like one delightfully long hug," Katy responded with a drowsy smile.

He quirked an eyebrow. "Katy? Are you falling asleep on me?"

"Mmm," she denied with a yawn. She could go on dancing with Derek forever, of course, but the combined effects of the wine, the traveling and the length of the day were proving to be too much. She didn't want to stop moving so sensually to the music, didn't want to pull away from the masculine strength of his embrace. But it was becoming more and more difficult for her to remain on her feet.

He shook his head with regret. "I forgot what a long day it's been for you." In an oddly tender gesture, he pressed his lips to her hair. "I'd better take you back to the hotel." Reluctantly Derek drew her away from the dance floor and back to their table. He called for the bill and quickly settled it. In another moment they had said their goodbyes to Mario, and not long afterward they were in a cab, on their way back to the hotel.

The effect of the fresh, night air during the drive in an open-windowed New York City taxi was somewhat reviving. By the time Derek walked her through the subdued lobby and over to the bank of elevators, Katy was no longer in a wine-induced haze. Nonetheless, he continued to keep a firm, guiding hand around her waist as he escorted her up the elevator and out into the hallway toward her room.

She fumbled in her purse for the key to the door. "I had a wonderful time," she murmured, inserting the brass key into the lock.

"I'm glad, honey." He seemed to tower above her. "As it happens, I had a pretty terrific time, myself."

There was a long pause, then the door clicked open. "I guess I'd better be getting to sleep, if I'm going to catch that flight back tomorrow morning."

"About that flight." Derek followed Katy into the room. "Why not stay a little longer?"

Katy looked up at him. "Oh, but I couldn't do that!"

He crossed his arms. "Why not?"

"Because," she stammered, "well, because I really should be getting home."

Derek gestured toward the window with its broad expanse of the city lights. "I thought *this* was your home, Katy."

There was a silence. "They're expecting me in Green Meadow tomorrow, Derek."

"I wonder, Katy—" there was a strange expression on his gaunt face "—will you be coming back at all?"

"Now that's a silly question, Derek Randall," she declared. "Of course I'll be back!"

There was something disquieting about the way Derek stood in the middle of the hotel room, as if he was waiting for something. But Katy was momentarily at a loss to discern just what that was. As he stood there, looking down at her, it almost seemed that he was intending to kiss her. But Katy couldn't be sure.

"I'd better let you get your rest," he finally said in a dull tone. "It's been a long day."

"Wait!" Katy exclaimed.

He stopped dead in his tracks. "What is it?"

"Before you go, Derek..." She paused. "I'd almost forgotten."

"Forgotten what?" There was almost an air of impatience in his demeanor.

How *could* she have forgotten! Katy was busy chastising herself. Hadn't she lugged that heavy package all the way down from Green Meadow? Didn't it take up so much room in her suitcase that she barely had room for a toothbrush? "I have something for you." She reached under the bed and pulled out the large box, gaily wrapped and completed with a festive blue bow.

"For *me*?" If a bomb had exploded outside, Derek could not have been more startled. "I don't understand."

"What's to understand?" Katy shrugged. "You know how seriously we take birthdays in Green Meadow. I owe you this one, Derek. I've never overlooked a birthday in my entire life."

Derek slowly sat down on the edge of the bed and lifted the box onto his lap. He continued to stare at the package in bewilderment. "You bought me a present?"

"Aren't you going to open it?" Katy asked gently.

"You didn't have to do this, Katy," he murmured, but inside he was flooded with a feeling of pleasure that this lovely young woman should care enough to even think about his birthday. For all his success and so-called "friends," gifts were not something that

Derek Randall received very often. "After all, what do you get the man who has everything?" people would remark with just the faintest hint of cynicism. Carefully he began to remove the striped gift wrap, somewhat curious to see exactly what Katy had bought for him.

Nothing, however, could have prepared him for the familiar lettering that slowly revealed itself as Derek tore away the foil paper. In vivid red across the top of the box were emblazoned the words The Casey Parking Garage and Filling Station. For a moment he was totally speechless. Derek simply stared down at the cardboard box in utter astonishment.

"Don't you like it?" Katy asked finally.

He shook his head wonderingly. "Where on earth . . . ? How did you ever find this?"

She hesitated. "First be honest and tell me if you like it."

"*Like* it?" Derek's features were transformed. "How can you even ask? Don't you realize what this is? It's Casey's Garage!" he exclaimed with a choke in his voice. He shook his head again in disbelief. "Still in the original cellophane wrapper, just like the one in the window. . . ." His words trailed off. There was the oddest expression in his silver eyes as he gingerly ran his tanned fingers across the top of the package. For the first time in his adult life, Derek Randall was very near to tears. Of course, there was no way he could ever let himself cry in front of anyone, particularly not this kind and beautiful creature. But when Derek looked back on it in later years, he would cherish this as one of the sweetest and most touching moments he had ever known. Slowly he set the box to one side and rose from the edge of the bed. "How could you manage to do such a wonderful thing?" In a matter of seconds, Derek practically towered over her. "Sweet, thoughtful, adorable Katy," he said and pulled her into his arms. "I always knew there was something magical about you!"

Katy suppressed a quiver. "There's no magic involved at all!" She tried to maintain a casual tone. "As it happens, the factory that manufactures the—"

Derek smiled and pressed a finger to her lips. "Tell me how you worked this miracle in a minute—all I want to do right now is thank you properly, darling!" He bent down and brushed his mouth with deliberate slowness against her cheeks, her forehead and whisper-softly against the delicate column of her throat. After each tantalizing caress, he murmured "Thank you," in a low whisper.

"You're welcome," came Katy's barely audible reply. She was still reeling, not only from those maddeningly brief kisses but from his unexpected endearment, as well. Being called "darling" by Derek Randall, even out of simple gratitude, was enough to cause a smile in her hopeful heart.

"Am I really *welcome*, Katy?" Derek gave the words a completely different implication. Before she could respond, he added the challenge, "Let's find out just how welcome I really am!" With a strange glitter in his eyes, he pulled her even more tightly against him. "I've been wanting to do this all day!" Now he sought out Katy's lips with a newfound urgency.

This kiss was not marked with the restraint that had characterized the previous ones. Derek coaxed her lips apart, invading her mouth with his moist, demanding warmth. "You're so sweet!" he exclaimed, "like honey!" His muscular thighs surged against her, making Katy aware of the extent of his arousal. How delicious to be molded so tightly against his male hardness, with every point of contact between them so electric! Derek's firm hands found and held Katy's hips. There was an almost shocking intimacy to this new embrace, but all Katy could do was give a happy sigh and yield even more willingly to the exquisite sensations he was evoking from her. Derek's eager tongue continued to probe and taste her many textures. And then his mouth finally left hers, traveling down the sensitive column of her throat in a trail of liquid fire.

"Oh, Derek!" she could only breathe, and strain her arms upward around his neck, her fingers savoring the smoothness of his short, brown hair. What a delectable kind of freedom, to be able to touch the man she loved with such proprietary gestures. Not that she would ever say the words aloud to Derek Randall. Not yet. For now, it was delicious just to feel his mouth possess her with such an unmistakable hunger. His hard hands moved down from her hips to linger on the feminine curve of her derriere. This was the most blatantly intimate of all Derek's caresses up to this point, and Katy was unable to suppress her response. "Derek!" she repeated involuntarily.

His voice was practically a growl. "Do you have any idea what I'd like to do to you right now, Katy?"

"Oh!" It was sheer heaven to hear him talk this way to her, for him to sound as if he wanted her in the most elemental way. But this sudden jumble of emotions, colliding headlong with physical sensations, was still all new to Katy.

Derek's mouth now sought out the tender flesh of her inner arm. "You're like silk, Katy! I know you must feel that way all over... pure silk and satin!"

The raw desire in his words made her shudder with exquisite anticipation. "You shouldn't talk that way!" she protested faintly.

"Why not?" His silver eyes raked her body with a possessiveness that made her feel completely undressed. "I'm only saying what's true!" Actually, it was driving Derek crazy to be holding her so closely. To feel her warm softness against him, and realize that for the first time since he had known Katy Kruger, they were utterly alone. No possible chance of interruption. No doorbells. No vicious Lorna to shatter his plans. No J. B. Halloran to intrude upon this intimate moment. At long last, he thought with supreme satisfaction, he had this exquisite young woman precisely where he wanted her. And despite her faint protests, Derek knew that Katy must want him almost as much as he craved her. Of course, she must! he reassured himself quickly. Why else would she have taken such incredible pains to find him this wonderful gift? In truth, there was no other present that Derek might have received, no item of clothing or expensive piece of jewelry that could more effectively have conveyed the intimacy of *this* delightfully unexpected offering.

It was absolutely unnecessary to "read" anything into Katy's giving of this present. As far as Derek was concerned, her message was strikingly clear. It was so very personal. And Derek's secret inner smile grew even broader. For there was no doubt in his mind as to exactly what was going to happen next.

"Come here, Katy," he demanded with a strange new light in his eyes. With total mastery he captured her willing mouth once more. But now Katy sensed that something was different. Something had changed. There was now something reckless, even dangerous about the way his hungry mouth seared its hot brand across the creamy expanse of flesh just below her collarbone. Deft fingers skillfully unfastened the top several buttons of the knit dress, and that same demanding mouth began to savor the shadowy hollow between her breasts.

Katy was speechless, unable to pull herself away from his devastating assault on her senses. In fact, she was quite unwilling to do so. She trembled as Derek gazed darkly at the swell of her breasts beneath the lacy pink material of her brassiere.

"Just let me touch you," he urged thickly, and ran a possessive hand over the pink silk. "Let me look at you, sweetheart!"

This endearment fell upon her ears like sweet rain, and Katy could only give a convulsive sigh of assent as Derek deftly unfastened the front clasp, exposing her naked breasts to his view. "You're so lovely, Katy—" he shook his head "—so exquisitely, unbelievably lovely!" With a groan he lowered his mouth to one rosy orb, taunting the tip to hardness, while his hands caressed the soft, sensitive flesh. Katy had never been touched so intimately before, but she clung to Derek without reserve, practically melting beneath his sensual onslaught. "Tell me you like it when I touch you, darling!" he whispered hotly. "Tell me!"

"Yes, Derek!"

"Yes, *what*?"

"I like it when you touch me," she breathed against his hair. What a heady, intoxicating feeling it was, to know that she could make a man want her this way.

"You're so pink and white," he marveled, tracing a delicate pattern around each perfect breast. "Like satin and velvet!" His tongue flicked maddeningly back and forth over the highly sensitized nipple.

Alarm bells began to go off inside Katy's head. Should she really be letting Derek touch her in this startlingly explicit way? It was obvious where such dangerously intimate love play could lead. "Derek, we shouldn't—"

"Of course we should," he murmured against her bare skin, and continued his tantalizingly erotic caresses.

"Please," Katy protested weakly. "This is going too far!"

Derek raised his head abruptly. "Going too far?" he repeated. "I thought you liked it when I touched you."

"I did. That is . . . I do, but—"

"But what?" There was a slight edge to his voice, where there hadn't been one before.

"It's just that—" She struggled with her conflicting emotions. Fear and desire battled within Katy. "It's just that everything is happening so . . . so fast!"

His taut features softened slightly. "Katy, it's not happening too fast. Not at all." He gave a gentle smile. "Not when it was always meant to happen between two people." He took her face in his hands. "Look at me, honey."

Katy gazed back at him, her eyes asking a silent question. "I am looking at you," she whispered.

"Good." Derek was thinking how lovely she was at that moment. Her cheeks were flushed, her red hair so exquisitely tousled and those eyes so luminous. Those beautiful eyes, with pupils dilated with desire. A desire for him that Katy could not conceal or even deny, no matter how much she might try. It was nearly impossible for Derek to even attempt to conceal the raging extent of his own desire. And come to think of it, why should he even try? His entire body shuddered with delicious anticipation. "Nothing can ever happen too fast. Not when it's something so unmistakably *right*. Between you and me, Katy, it would have to be perfect!" He planted a trail of butterfly kisses along the tender line of her nape. "Besides—" his voice was deep and smoothly persuasive "—it isn't happening too quickly at all, you know. It seems as if I've been waiting forever for this!" Derek's words were a soothing, sensual balm. It was a subtle kind of seduction in itself, to be made so utterly aware how much this man had desired her, right from the very start. To be told by the person she loved that he felt an absolute *rightness* in both of them being together, those were the very words Katy wanted to hear. Only the words "I love you..." could have given her a greater joy at this moment. Of course, she thought with a bittersweet tinge, *that* would be asking for the moon. For now it was enough just to know that Derek needed and wanted her.

"Do you have any idea how long I've waited for this?" His silver gaze raked her body with shocking boldness. "Oh, Katy, don't you know what you're doing to me?" Without waiting for a response, Derek gathered her up in his arms and carried her across the room.

"What . . . what are you doing?" Katy's voice was nearly inaudible.

"I thought that was obvious," he murmured against her scented skin. "I'm taking you to bed!"

He deposited her on top of the quilted coverlet with incredible tenderness, pausing long enough to brush a stray wisp of hair from her forehead. Then Derek impatiently tugged off his elegant woolen jacket and tossed it onto the carpet. He hastily pulled away his silk tie, as well. Seconds later he rejoined Katy, his weight sinking into the mattress. For the briefest space of time he just stared at her in wonderment. "My sweet, lovely Katy!" he uttered thickly, "I want to see all of you!" Before she could even protest, Derek had unfastened the remaining buttons of her dress and unhooked the leather belt with experienced fingers. In another moment, the garment was being skillfully slipped down over her hips and then past the smooth flesh of her thighs. "There should be no barriers between us," he rasped, and impatiently began to strip away the rest of her silken lingerie. But when his fingers began to pull at the lacy scalloped waistband of her panties, Katy instinctively reached up and stilled Derek's hands.

"Don't."

He paused, those enigmatic eyes studying her flushed cheeks and the way Katy averted her gaze. "Can you really be that shy?" came the slow question. "One might think you've never been undressed by a man before."

Katy gave a nervous laugh. "What makes you say that?"

Derek caressed the gentle curve of her bare thigh. "Never mind that now. Just let me touch you, sweetheart!" With determined fingers, he deftly removed the last offending undergarment. Looking down at her completely naked body, he drew in his breath. "You're perfect. Absolutely exquisite—just as I imagined you'd be!" His rugged, angular features were softened with passion, the once-harsh face now aglow with the anticipation of a fulfillment yet to come. Derek's pulse rate continued to climb as he devoured her with his eyes, and he gave an involuntary groan. "I'll make it so wonderful for you, Katy! You won't be sorry, I promise!"

She shook her head. "I could never be sorry, Derek." *Because I love you!* Katy wanted to cry out, but she bit back the words that trembled on her lips. Later on, after this wonderful man had made love to her, after he had unlocked all the sweet secrets of her womanhood, then she could trust her feelings. In the sweet aftermath of passion, Katy would be free to tell Derek everything she longed for him to know. There would be no barriers left.

"Come here," Derek challenged softly. She felt a dark thrill shiver through her senses. "This time, you kiss *me*, honey!"

Katy paused for just an instant, then threw caution to the wind. She wrapped her bare arms around his neck and drew Derek's head toward her. Katy pressed her lips to his rough cheeks, his eyelids, the jagged line of that white scar. And then, as he quivered visibly, she brought her mouth directly onto his.

Derek gave a low moan and began to answer her kisses. His own mouth took over Katy's tentative exploration and started a ruthless onslaught of its own. He needed to taste every inch of her, and hungry lips ravaged Katy's throat, her shoulders and her breasts. Derek spent long, lingering moments suckling the pink tip of each orb, before moving lower down to the satiny skin of her flat stomach. "You taste so good!" he groaned.

Katy burned beneath his heated caresses. The pleasure created by his touch was so intense, she could hardly bear it any longer. Derek's mouth traveled back to her lips once more. When he parted those lips in a kiss of shattering intimacy, plundering the sweet moistness of her willing mouth, the tremors of passion racked both of their bodies, creating shock waves everywhere. And now Katy knew she could no longer deny herself the ultimate fulfillment. "Show me what to do, Derek!" she gasped.

"My sweet Katy—" his voice practically cracked "—you already know!"

Locking her in his heated embrace, he pressed her back against the pillows. His hands were everywhere, setting her body aflame. Then he pulled back and reached for the belt of his trousers. In another moment, the rest of his expensive, tailored garments joined the pile already discarded on the floor. Then Derek slowly positioned himself over Katy, his taut, hard body pressed against her feminine softness.

"Derek!" Katy gasped in a voice that wasn't her own.

His eyes glinted down at her. "Don't worry, darling. Trust me and I'll take care of everything."

But he was quite unprepared for the adoration on Katy's face as she gazed up at him with a bright smile. "Of course I trust you," she said simply.

The sweet tone of her reply touched Derek as nothing else could. What had he done to deserve this? Never had he dreamed that a woman could be so soft, so desirable or so very trusting. At this moment he was in heaven. In a few brief minutes, Katy would be completely and utterly his. "I'll be very careful, honey," he assured her gently. "I won't get you pregnant."

Instinctively Katy stiffened. This was something she hadn't even considered. "I'm not worried," she answered faintly. In truth, she was thinking that to have a baby with Derek Randall would be the most beautiful thing that could ever happen to her.

He stared at her strangely. "Oh," he remarked in a slightly pained tone. "Of course. I forgot that you and J.B. would certainly use precautions."

Katy's body became even more tense beneath his. Before she could stop herself, the words were out of her mouth. "J.B. and I don't use precautions!" she practically shouted. "J.B. and I don't *use* anything...for the simple reason that J.B. and I don't *do* anything!"

Derek's silver gaze narrowed. "Do you mean to tell me that you and he aren't—?"

"He and I most certainly are *not*!" Katy was almost adamant. Was that what he actually believed? That she had been sleeping with the handsome sheriff of Green Meadow?

"Is that the truth?" he demanded.

Her anger escalated. "Oh, I'll give you the truth, Mr. Derek Randall!" she continued in a careless fury. "I have never been intimately involved with J. B. Halloran—or anyone else, for that matter!"

There was an odd silence. "What do you mean by that?" Derek said slowly.

Oh, damn, Katy thought. Why hadn't she stopped the reckless revelation, before it had escaped her lips? This was the old chestnut about being caught between a rock and a hard place. Either let Derek keep believing that she was an experienced woman, courtesy of J. B. Halloran, or allow him to know the simple truth. She was completely without sexual experience. Some choice!

"I said, what do you mean by that?" Derek repeated hoarsely. "What do you mean you've never been 'intimately' involved with anyone?"

She shrugged uneasily. "It's not a big deal."

"The hell it's not!" he practically boomed. "Damn it, Katy, just tell me! Are you still a virgin?"

"Why is that so important—?"

Derek's jaw tightened. "Don't prevaricate. Just give me an answer!"

She gave a weary sigh. "Oh, all right. Not that it matters—"

"An *answer*, Katy!" His tone was ominous.

"So what if I *am* still a virgin?" she protested.

The blood drained from Derek's face. "Oh, God!"

"Now, just a minute, Derek Randall!" Katy declared with some degree of indignance. "Why are you suddenly so horrified?"

"When, exactly, did you intend to tell me?" he demanded harshly. There was an uncomfortable pause. "Or did you just decide to let nature take its course?"

"What does that matter? You would have found out, one way or the other."

"Oh, it matters." He ground out the words. "It matters a hell of a lot, in fact!" Derek quickly rolled his tense body away from hers and began to search for his clothes.

"What are you doing?"

"What does it look like I'm doing?" he practically growled. "I'm getting dressed."

"Why?"

"I should think that was obvious, Katy." Derek hastily zipped up his trousers, then reached for the white oxford shirt. "What kind of experience do you think making love would have been, if we hadn't stopped?" The man's voice actually shook. "I wouldn't have known about your innocence until it was too late, Katy. I wouldn't have known to be extra gentle." His eyes darkened. "Do you have any idea how painful and unpleasant it might have been for you?" Derek paused bitterly. "Do you have any idea what it would have done to me, to hurt you like that?"

"Derek." She reached out a conciliatory hand.

"And for heaven's sake, cover yourself!" He drew the sheets over Katy's completely naked body.

"Why are you acting this way?" Katy was stunned at his sudden change in demeanor. A moment ago, Derek Randall had been wild and out of control, a master at the art of seduction. Now he was prudish and withdrawn. It was as if all the passion and sensual abandon had never even happened. Where was the man who had trembled with desire in her arms? Who was this aloof, cold-eyed stranger who had taken his place? "Does it change things so much?" she finally asked in a low voice.

Derek fastened his other gold cuff link and stared back at Katy, sitting so dejectedly in the queen-size bed. Her hair still tumbled over her bare shoulders, and her lips were still soft and bruised from his kisses, but her once-luminous eyes were dull and lifeless. Never, in all the time he had known her, had Derek ever seen Katy look so hurt and miserable. Knowing that *he* had been the cause of her pain made Derek even angrier with himself than he already was. Stifling an oath, he leaned over and pulled her roughly into his arms. "Yes, honey—" Derek shook his head "—it changes things very much." He pressed his lips tenderly against her forehead. "More than you could possibly ever know."

"Are you saying that you don't want me anymore?"

Derek's heart froze at the pain in Katy's voice. Was he responsible for this? "You don't understand," he exclaimed. "I want you so badly that I ache, honey!"

Some of the tension seemed to leave her body. "You do, Derek?"

Katy sounded so happy that Derek wanted to jump ten feet into the air. What a revelation this was! He'd had no idea that Katy had cared this much. "I ache for you right now," he confessed openly.

She brightened visibly, a new luster in her lovely green eyes. "Is that true?"

With considerable restraint, Derek's hard, tanned fingers pulled away the bed sheet to reveal Katy's nude body. "Just look at you, sweetheart!" he groaned agonizingly. "You're so damn beautiful. It's taking every ounce of self-control I have, not to—"

Katy's mouth trembled. "Not to what?"

Hastily Derek covered her with the sheet again. He cleared his throat. "We'll talk about this at another time." Derek rose from the bed abruptly. "I'd better be going now."

"Why can't we talk about this now, Derek?" she insisted in puzzlement. Katy just didn't understand. Why was he acting this way?

He smiled ironically. "Trust me. This isn't the time for us to do any more talking." There was a long pause. "Have you ever heard the expression 'trying to do the right thing'?" He twisted his mouth. "I'm trying to do the right thing here, and Lord, it isn't easy!"

Realization flooded her somewhat belatedly. "Is it possible, Mr. Randall, that you've suddenly become old-fashioned?"

No one in Derek's circle of acquaintances would ever have believed that he could gaze at a woman with such infinite patience and tenderness. And Derek himself would never have believed that he would ever willingly leave the bed of a lovely, desirable young woman without actually making love to her first. Certainly not a young woman who had haunted all his fantasies since the moment of their first meeting.

"Katy," he murmured quietly, "when it comes to you, I am decidedly old-fashioned!"

What did he mean, though, she kept wondering, about the "right thing"? Katy was still unclear. Was this all just Derek's way of being noble, because she

was a virgin? Men were so uptight about such a con-
dition, she'd always heard. Still, it was somewhat de-
flating to remember that in all this talk of self-control
and desire and being old-fashioned, not a single word
of love had passed between them. This was a sobering
realization, indeed. But there it was, she reminded
herself. Never once had Derek mentioned the word
"love." And amid all this talk of being "old-
fashioned" where it concerned her, neither had the
man mentioned marriage. Her heart sank. What had
she expected? Just because you loved a man didn't
automatically mean he had to love you back. Had she
expected some kind of declaration of love in the intimacy of the moment? A proposal of marriage? After
all, Katy recalled bitterly, this was a man who was used
to worldly, sophisticated women. He'd probably never
had to deal with a virgin before. She hadn't fully appreciated what an awkward and bewildering situation
it might be for him. Not to mention embarrassing.

She forced a bittersweet smile to her lips. "You're
quite right, of course. This really isn't the time to discuss it."

"I'm glad you agree." Derek sighed.

"It is better for you to go now." She tried to mask
the disappointment in her voice.

"Get a good night's sleep, honey." He searched her
face, trying to find the answer to a question he hadn't
even dared ask himself yet. "We'll talk this all over at
breakfast."

"Breakfast?" Katy repeated, as if she'd never heard of the word.

"I'll come by at eight o'clock." Derek tucked his silk tie into his jacket pocket.

"That really isn't necessary," she replied hastily. "Anyhow, I doubt there will be time, with my flight and all."

"Flight? What the hell are you talking about?"

Katy bit her lower lip tremulously. "I've got a flight back to Green Meadow in the morning. Don't you remember?"

"I remember everything." He glanced at her sharply. "But as far as your returning to Green Meadow in the morning goes, just forget it. You aren't going anywhere."

Her heart thundered in her chest. "Who are you to tell me what I can and cannot do? Everybody is expecting me home tomorrow, Derek."

His eyes narrowed to icy silver. "Well, then they'll just be disappointed, won't they? Because you're staying right where you are until we talk about this, Katy Kruger." He reached down to the floor, retrieved the gift package and stared at it for a moment.

"And don't think you can give that back, either!" she called out. "You're stuck with that hunk of scrap metal, Derek Randall."

"I certainly hope so," he retorted. "It's the best present I've ever gotten in my life." He stalked over to the bed, leaned over and kissed her hard on the mouth. "We *will* talk later, Katy." His eyes raked her body, now partially concealed beneath the sheet, with blatant possessiveness. "You can count on that."

Without another word, he turned and walked quickly from the room.

Katy could only stare after him in utter confusion. She sat there in bed, her legs hunched up to her chest, lost in thought until it was daylight.

Chapter Ten

When Derek Randall returned to his apartment that night, he was unable to shake the image of Katy lying against him in an intimate embrace. Although leaving her like that, when she was so lovely and willing, was the most excruciatingly painful thing he had ever done in his life, Derek knew it had also been the wisest. Katy had given him two gifts tonight, each wonderful and rare in its own right. The first one sat on his dresser table. The second, however, was something far more precious. Katy had offered the gift of herself. It was a unique treasure, the likes of which Derek had never been offered before. There could be nothing quite so touching and rare as the gift of innocence. And that was what Katy had been willing to give so freely. It was something he could never have expected in his wildest dreams. It had simply never occurred to Derek that someone of Katy's vivaciousness and beauty could possibly still be a virgin at the age of twenty-four. He could imagine all the opportunities she must have had, and yet allowed to pass by. And then, of course, there was J. B. Halloran. Incredible as it might seem, she had also passed him by, as well.

Derek stared into the mirror, taking in his less than dazzling appearance. What on earth did Katy see in him? He wasn't what women ever referred to as handsome, he reminded himself for the thousandth time. A permanent weariness was etched on his gaunt features. His profile was marred by a crooked nose, smashed back when he'd been a teenager, in the same street fight that had also scarred his cheek. Growing up in the toughest neighborhood in Philadelphia, it had been hard to avoid confrontations. But the roughneck who had accosted him in the alley that night with a broken bottle had been searching for someone to confront. It didn't matter that he was a virtual stranger. Derek sighed. The point was that Katy Kruger could have her choice of handsome young men, and yet she had chosen him, when it came time to bestow a woman's most precious treasure. How could such a thing be, when they had only known each other such a short time?

Derek turned away from the mirror. He could never look at his harsh facial features for very long. What did it mean, he marveled, when a young woman saved herself for a man? But even as his heart leaped, he already knew the answer. It sparkled in a million bright lights onto his consciousness. As unbelievable as it might seem, the reason a woman like Katy offered herself to a man was because of one thing and one thing alone. *Love.* She loved him! That was what it had to be! And Derek could only sigh with utter amazement. He'd never even used the word "love" before; it had always seemed like such a remote possibility for him. Derek smiled broadly now. The secret inner smile was no longer a mystery. At long last, Derek Randall had finally decoded its meaning.

At five o'clock in the morning, restless and unable to fall asleep, Derek rose from his bed and decided to assemble the metal parts of Casey's Parking Garage. As he sat cross-legged on the bedroom floor and began to tear away the cellophane wrapper, he noticed, for the first time, the tiny print on one side of the cardboard box. "Casey's Parking Garage and Gas Station," the tiny label read. "Manufactured expressly for Lombard's Department Store by K.T.W., Green Meadow, New York." There was the oddest sensation in the pit of Derek's stomach. After the first reaction of surprise came a feeling of utter inevitability that it should all have led back to Green Meadow. There was a magic to everything associated with Katy Kruger, her grandfather and the town of Green

Meadow. And K.T.W.—the Kruger Toy Works. It was as if he'd turned over the last page of a complex mystery novel and found all his questions answered, at long last. In a blinding flash of light, Derek Randall's outlook shifted one hundred eighty degrees.

At eight o'clock in the morning, Derek called Katy, told her he would be late for breakfast and asked her to wait for him.

At eight-thirty, Derek sat in the packed executive boardroom of Consolidated Industries and unveiled his new plan to produce a line of quality high-end toys, utilizing the facilities of the Kruger Toy Works. These items would be reproduced down to the last detail, with painstaking accuracy, using the original molds and specifications, under the supervision of the toys' manufacturer and designer, Mr. Leo Kruger.

"I don't know about this, Derek." Morgan Strickland shook his head with a small degree of hesitation. "You're the one who keeps saying how unstable the toy market is."

Derek pressed his lips together. "It appears to me, after extensive research and analysis, that the market for adult-oriented nostalgia toys is wide open, a vast potential just waiting for us to tap." He paused. "But if Consolidated isn't interested in pursuing this particular course, I'd be perfectly willing to find independent funding elsewhere." He used the intimidatingly cool tone that had shriveled many an objection in his professional life here at Consolidated.

"Oh, you're bluffing, Derek," interjected Les Winters with a cynical cough.

"Try me."

The smile Derek wore when he arrived at Katy's room at eleven-thirty was bright enough to light up the sky. He handed her a bouquet of pink roses, crossed his arms and said, "I have something to tell you, Katy."

She stared up at the man who had left the hotel room so abruptly the evening before. Was this the same Derek Randall, who now looked ten years younger, as if the worry and tension had left his eyes forever?

"I called your grandfather about fifteen minutes ago. He's going to be flying down in the morning. I've arranged for him to meet with the president of Consolidated to discuss a full-scale retooling of the Kruger Toy Works."

Katy stood there, a picture of utter bewilderment in her green dress and even greener eyes. "I don't understand—"

"There's a wonderful market out there, Katy. A vast, untapped gold mine of children in their thirtie and forties—"

"Children?"

Derek smiled. "Yes, sweetheart. We're all children, no matter how old we become. I learned that last night. *You* taught it to me." He drew her into his arms. "I have to thank you for giving me back something I thought I'd lost forever. The wonder of childhood."

"I think I understand now," she ventured. "You think it's possible to reissue some of the original toys, the way they were produced the first time?"

"That's the *hook*, as they say. Using the same quality materials . . . the pressed steel, the hard vinyl, and taking advantage of all the wonderful workers up in Green Meadow who were on the original assembly line."

Katy could hardly keep back the tears. "Do you realize what that could do for our town?"

"Yes, I do," Derek answered quietly, his silver gaze locked with hers. "Your grandfather was most effusive on the subject, when I spoke to him. But he'll tell you all about it, when you see him tomorrow."

There was something else going on here, Katy sensed. But what was it? Derek's eyes kept probing her face, looking for the answer to an unspoken question. "Uh—" She felt the need to say something to cover her sudden nervousness. "That's pretty quick, isn't it? Gramps is going to meet with your people tomorrow?"

Derek quirked a curious eyebrow. "I never said that."

Katy placed her hands on her hips, trying to ignore the tantalizing sensation of Derek's hard hands on her shoulders. "Yes, I distinctly heard you say he was meeting with your president tomorrow."

Derek's mouth twisted. "No, honey. All I said was that he'd be flying down in the morning. He can meet with Morgan anytime he wants."

"Derek Randall, you're confusing the devil out of me!"

"Am I?" he murmured against her ear. "I want to confuse you, Katy. I want you as bewitched, hot and bothered as you make me!"

His confession was so startling that Katy could only flush a bright pink and stare up at him in amazement. "What are you saying to me?"

"You bewitch me, Katy." His mouth pressed against her whisper-soft cheek. "And I think it's time we did something about it."

Katy swallowed convulsively, leaning against his hard, lean strength. "What would you suggest?" she replied in a voice that was strangely high-pitched.

"Oh, I don't know." Derek shrugged. "Maybe we could go down to city hall on Friday and get married, or something."

"What?" Katy practically shouted.

"Don't look so shocked, sweetheart. When I mentioned the idea to your grandfather, he seemed to like it just fine. In fact, that happens to be the reason he's flying down in the morning."

"I don't believe this! You told my grandfather—?" She raged, then stopped. What was she raging about? Wasn't this what she'd always wanted? What she'd dreamed of? To be Derek Randall's wife?

"I'm crazy in love with you, sweetheart," Derek confessed softly, "and if I'm not mistaken, I have the feeling it's mutual."

"Oh—" she sighed raggedly "—it's most definitely mutual."

"Then let me hear you say it, Katy," Derek demanded.

"I love you," she breathed.

Derek's arms closed around her slender form. "It never occurred to me that you might even feel this way until a few hours ago, honey." He sought her lips with his own, savoring her response to his caresses. "What kind of honeymoon would you like?"

"It doesn't matter." She pressed her face against the soft cotton of his shirt and inhaled his fresh, masculine aroma. "Anywhere at all."

"After we're married, I'll be spending quite a bit of time up in Green Meadow, helping set up the operation with your grandfather." He smiled faintly. "It sounds like a pretty lovely summer, Katy."

"It certainly does." She was lost in the delirious joy of knowing that all her dreams were coming true. This wonderful man loved her, and wanted to marry her. Prosperity would come to Green Meadow again, and her grandfather would be doing what he loved best in the world...making his delightfully original toys. Yes, the summer ahead promised so much joy and enchantment. She could hardly wait for it to begin.

"Speaking of honeymoons—" a curious shudder racked Derek's body "—I've been thinking, Katy." His voice was oddly unsteady.

"Yes, Derek?" She smiled knowingly.

"Do you suppose we could start our honeymoon now?"

Katy smiled her own secret inner smile, and wrapped her arms about her future husband's neck. "I thought you'd never ask," she whispered, even as he lifted her into his arms.

* * * * *

COMING NEXT MONTH

#658 A WOMAN IN LOVE—Brittany Young
When archaeologist Melina Chase met the mysterious Aristo Drapano aboard a treasure-hunting ship in the Greek isles, she knew he was her most priceless find....

#659 WALTZ WITH THE FLOWERS—Marcine Smith
When Estella Blaine applied for a loan to build a stable on her farm, she never expected bank manager Cody Marlowe to ask for her heart as collateral!

#660 IT HAPPENED ONE MORNING—Jill Castle
A chance encounter in the park with free-spirited dog trainer Collier Woolery had Neysa Williston's orderly heart spinning. Could he convince her that their meeting was destiny?

#661 DREAM OF A LIFETIME—Arlene James
Businessman Dan Wilson needed an adventure and found one in the Montana Rockies with lovely mountain guide Laney Scott. But now he wanted her to follow his trail....

#662 THE WEDDING MARCH—Terry Essig
Feisty five-foot Lucia Callahan had had just about enough of tall, protective men, and she set out to find a husband her own size...but she couldn't resist Daniel Statler—all six feet of him!

#663 NO WAY TO TREAT A LADY—Rita Rainville
Aunt Tillie was at it again, matchmaking between her llama-ranching nephew, Dave McGraw, and reading teacher Jennifer Hale. True love would never be the same again!

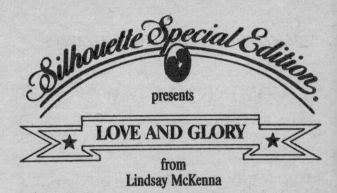

Silhouette Special Edition

presents

★ LOVE AND GLORY ★

from
Lindsay McKenna

Introducing a gripping new series celebrating our men—and women—in uniform. Meet the Trayherns, a military family as proud and colorful as the American flag, a family fighting the shadow of dishonor, a family determined to triumph—with **LOVE AND GLORY!**

June: A QUESTION OF HONOR (SE #529) leads the fast-paced excitement. When Coast Guard officer Noah Trayhern offers Kit Anderson a safe house, he unwittingly endangers his own guarded emotions.

July: NO SURRENDER (SE #535) Navy pilot Alyssa Trayhern's assignment with arrogant jet jockey Clay Cantrell threatens her career—and her heart—with a crash landing!

August: RETURN OF A HERO (SE #541) Strike up the band to welcome home a man whose top-secret reappearance will make headline news . . . with a delicate, daring woman by his side.

"GIVE YOUR HEART TO SILHOUETTE" SWEEPSTAKES
OFFICIAL RULES
NO PURCHASE NECESSARY TO ENTER OR RECEIVE A PRIZE

o enter and join the Silhouette Reader Service, rub off the concealment device on all game tickets. This will reveal the potential value for each Sweepstakes entry number and the number of free book(s) you will receive. Accepting the free book(s) will automatically entitle you to also receive a free bonus gift. If you do not wish to take advantage of our introduction to the Silhouette Reader Service but wish to enter the Sweepstakes only, rub off the concealment device on tickets #1-3 only. To enter, return your entire sheet of tickets. Incomplete and/or inaccurate entries are not eligible for that section or section (s) of prizes. Not responsible for mutilated or unreadable entries or inadvertent printing errors. Mechanically reproduced entries are null and void.

Either way, your Sweepstakes numbers will be compared against the list of winning numbers generated at random by computer. In the event that all prizes are not claimed, random drawings will be made from all entries received from all presentations to award all unclaimed prizes. All cash prizes are payable in U.S. funds. This is in addition to any free, surprise or mystery gifts that might be offered. The following prizes are awarded in this sweepstakes:

(1)	*Grand Prize	$1,000,000	Annuity
(1)	First Prize	$35,000	
(1)	Second Prize	$10,000	
(3)	Third Prize	$5,000	
(10)	Fourth Prize	$1,000	
(25)	Fifth Prize	$500	
(5000)	Sixth Prize	$5	

The Grand Prize is payable through a $1,000,000 annuity. Winner may elect to receive $25,000 a year for 40 years, totaling up to $1,000,000 without interest, or $350,000 in one cash payment. Winners selected will receive the prizes offered in the Sweepstakes promotion they receive.

Entrants may cancel the Reader Service privileges at any time without cost or obligation to buy (see details in your insert card).

Versions of this Sweepstakes with different graphics may be offered in other mailings or at retail outlets by Torstar Corp. and its affiliates. This promotion is being conducted under the supervision of Marden-Kane, Inc., an independent judging organization. By entering this Sweepstakes, each entrant accepts and agrees to be bound by these rules and the decisions of the judges, which shall be final and binding. Odds of winning are dependent upon the total number of entries received. Taxes, if any, are the sole responsibility of the winners. Prizes are nontransferable. All entries must be received by March 31, 1990. The drawing will take place on April 30, 1990, at the offices of Marden-Kane, Inc., Lake Success, N.Y.

This offer is open to residents of the U.S., Great Britain and Canada, 18 years or older, except employees of Torstar Corp., its affiliates, and subsidiaries, Marden-Kane, Inc. and all other agencies and persons connected with conducting this Sweepstakes. All federal, state and local laws apply. Void wherever prohibited or restricted by law.

Winners will be notified by mail and may be required to execute an affidavit of eligibility and release that must be returned within 14 days after notification. Canadian winners will be required to answer a skill-testing question. Winners consent to the use of their name, photograph and/or likeness for advertising and publicity in conjunction with this and similar promotions without additional compensation. One prize per family or household.

For a list of our most current major prizewinners, send a stamped, self-addressed envelope to: WINNERS LIST, c/o MARDEN-KANE, INC., P.O. BOX 701, SAYREVILLE, N.J. 08871

If sweepstakes entry form is missing, please print your name and address on a 3" ×5" piece of plain paper and send to:

In the U.S.	In Canada
Sweepstakes Entry	Sweepstakes Entry
901 Fuhrmann Blvd.	P.O. Box 609
P.O. Box 1867	Fort Erie, Ontario
Buffalo, NY 14269-1867	L2A 5X3

LTY-S69R